ISBN 978-1-331-19407-1
PIBN 10156714

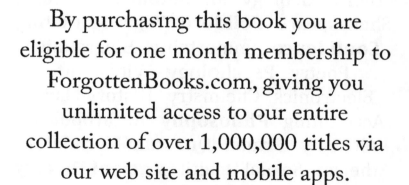

English
Français
Deutsche
Italiano
Español
Português

www.forgottenbooks.com

Mythology Photography **Fiction**
Fishing Christianity **Art** Cooking
Essays Buddhism Freemasonry
Medicine **Biology** Music **Ancient**
Egypt Evolution Carpentry Physics
Dance Geology **Mathematics** Fitness
Shakespeare **Folklore** Yoga Marketing
Confidence Immortality Biographies
Poetry **Psychology** Witchcraft
Electronics Chemistry History **Law**
Accounting **Philosophy** Anthropology
Alchemy Drama Quantum Mechanics
Atheism Sexual Health **Ancient History**
Entrepreneurship Languages Sport
Paleontology Needlework Islam
Metaphysics Investment Archaeology
Parenting Statistics Criminology
Motivational

NARRATIVE,

OF

EDMUND WRIGHT;

HIS ADVENTURES WITH AND ESCAPE FROM

THE KNIGHTS OF THE GOLDEN CIRCLE.

"Truth is Stranger than Fiction."

CINCINNATI:

J. R. HAWLEY, 164 VINE STREET.

1864.

CONTENTS.

CHAPTER I.

CHAPTER II.

CHAPTER III.

CHAPTER IV.

CHAPTER V.

CHAPTER VI.

CHAPTER VII.

CHAPTER VIII.

CHAPTER IX.

CHAPTER X.

CHAPTER XI.

CHAPTER XII.

CONTENTS.

CHAPTER XIII.

CHAPTER XIV.

CHAPTER XV.

CHAPTER XVI.

CHAPTER XVII.

CHAPTER XVIII.

CHAPTER XIX.

CHAPTER XX.

CHAPTER XXI.

ASTOUNDING DISCLOSURES!

TEMPLES

OF THE

K. G. C. UNVAILED.

CHAPTER I.

Introduction—Love of Right—The Author acquires his Education in the North
—He Marries a Yankee Woman—Takes her to the Sunny South—Finds
His Father a Knight—The Author Bitten by the Snake—Opinions of other
Victims—The Serpent Jewel—Illinois Copperheads—Spies in the North—
Reuben Stout—Atrocities of the Order—Court of Saint Hive.

In the course of every man's career through life, opportunities
are presented to him, when, if embraced, he may enlighten his
fellow-man.

The school of experience is a hard one, and has been most essentially so to the writer. Still, the hard lessons he has learned will
not deter him from imparting to his fellow-men the knowledge he
has acquired.

Throwing aside all other lessons learned, some most pleasurable
and others equally abhorrent to my innate love of right, I at once
essay a theme, which duty to myself, mankind and my country, im-
pels me to perform.

"The Knights of the Golden Circle."—To add to the imperfect history and workings of this institution already given to the
world, I, who blush that it was my misfortune to have been lured
into the meshes of the most damnable organization ever conceived
of outside of the lowest depths of pollution, propose to enter the
inner temple, in which I have been time and again, and portray a
few of the horrid scenes there witnessed.

Before fully encountering the task I have planned, in my mind, it may not be amiss to say a word or two as to myself.

Born of parents whose lot had been cast in a Southern section of this once great and happy Republic, and whose forefathers, from the days of the Revolution, had been honored with, and had given honor to, the high positions they held, by men whose offspring are now in open rebellion against the Union of their fathers' love, I passed the earlier years of my life in the Sunny South. Atlanta, Georgia, was the place of my birth; a pretty little town, and will so continue, unless the blight of secession overshadows it with its all-pervading curse. The circumstances of my father enabled him to give me an opportunity to acquire an education and to " see the world."

In those days, to visit Charleston and New Orleans was the hight of my ambition. The visit to both was made, and I returned home. On the part of my mother it was suggested that I had not yet seen enough of the world, and that by all means I should go North and see the outside barbarians, called "Yankees." Well, suffice it to say, I went to the " land of steady habits," to learn, or rather to teach the people there what we knew in the South, but at once I found I knew nothing.

Disgusted with my ignorance, of which I felt conscious, I determined to remain in the North until I could hear from home. I visited Fanuiel Hall, the libraries and other noble institutions of Boston ; took a trip to the Empire City, looked into some of her great manufactories, saw the shipping of her port, and wondered where all the boxes of dry goods, hardware and many other manufactures, came from, especially as I was impressed with the belief that to my native South all America, if not all the world, was indebted for everything useful, needful or luxurious.

Time rolled on, and remittances reached me from home, with permission to remain in the North awhile, if I thought I was adding to my store of knowledge. I thought so, especially as I had acquired a very good knowledge of the fair and intellectual daughter of a "Yankee." Enough, we were married. She wished to see the Sunny South, and so did I. In a week or two she saw her mother-in-law, and I my mother; but my father was not at home. He was on a visit, as mother informed me, to a conclave of the K. G. C. in a neighboring town.

To me K. G. C. was all Greek.

"You will have to join the order," says mother. "Your father will expect it, and so will all your friends."

Before I had time to reply to mother, the door opened and in rushed my father. Though I at once recognized him, I was forcibly struck with his manner and appearance. When I left home he was sedate, affable and courteous to all; now he appeared a being wholly unlike his former self.

" Got back, Ned, have you?" was his first salutation.

I arose, offered him one hand, and with the other drew my wife from her seat, and introduced her to him.

" Been getting married, have you. Hope you haven't brought any Abolition woman to disgrace our family."

I told him that, though she was of a Northern family, neither she nor they were Abolitionists.

"Don't talk nonsense to me; all Yankees are Abolitionists, and it has been so decided by our noble order of K. G. C. You must join the order at once, or I will disinherit you. Will you do so at our next meeting?"

Totally ignorant of the character and purposes of the organization, I, without hesitation, assented. Then was it that I fell into the coils of the venomous serpent, which soon, as I will relate, held me as a charmed bird within its baleful influence, until, by the blessing of God and the glorious impressions implanted in my bosom while in the North, I burst the accursed fetters, and once more stand erect as an American freeman, with the full determination to expose, so far as in me lies, the hell-engendered machinations, orgies and purposes of that disgrace upon civilization, Christianity and decency; that emanation from the arch-fiend himself, when, in his bitterest mood, he would avenge his fall from the presence of the Almighty—I mean the organization known to devils, and alas! to men, as

" THE KNIGHTS OF THE GOLDEN CIRCLE."

Induced, as I have already stated, in an unguarded moment, I consented to become a " Knight," and through the influence of my father I was readily admitted to membership in the initiatory degree of the order. Step by step I advanced until the goal of infamy had been attained. In my soul I was fully convinced that the career I was pursuing was most infamous; but, having entered upon it, I determined to pursue it to the bitter end; and the proud satisfaction I now have is to atone for my error and persistence therein, by thus warning others against falling into the infernal vortex that engulfed me, until the light of returning reason enabled me to escape from that sink of iniquity.

As it is the intention of the writer, to defer for future chapters of his hastily written work, an exposition of the origin, purposes, rites, ceremonies and iniquities of the hell-begotten bands, who, in numerous localities constitute the Golden Circle, he proposes to prelude the leading subject matter of the book, with a few details of others, who, like himself, were ensnared by the serpent.

An intelligent friend having learned that this work was in the course of preparation, has handed the following, as a hastily written statement of his experience with the " Knights :"

" Having been a sufferer in everything by which pain can be inflicted upon weak humanity, and all attributable to that hell-born legion of the Knights of the Golden Circle, who accomplished the destruction of my home, and were the cause, fell and accursed, of the murder of my wife and infant boy, a brother and a dear friend; I believe I would be held recreant to manhood, did I not lay bare many facts which occurred in the immediate vicinity in which I lived for several years. The atrocious and damnable deeds practised upon the unwary, weak and inoffensive people, who stood in the path over which these fell destroyers stalked, appals my every sense, even now, when my bitterest woes have been somewhat temporized by the hand of time, in its slow progress toward eternity. A sense of duty, like an incumbent necessity, demands that I should expose most fully, the infernal machinations which the Knights of the Circle employ to entrap their victims, or to ensnare those whom they afterward employ as mere tools, with which they inflict tortures upon all those who are opponents to this association; whose compact is a deed of horrid darkness, and one of such a desperate nature, that no man possessing a spark of virtue, could believe it born of earth.

" Far and wide have these so-called Knights and their emissaries, traveled over this once happy land, planting their castles wherever the blighting cause of secession found advocates, and, like the serpent that charms its prey, the more readily to secure its capture, they have allured thousands of good but unwary men, into their meshes of destruction, from which but few escape. Take heed then, men of America, and be counseled, for these fiends are around and about you, gnawing at the very vitals of your liberties. You may not have seen its sycophantic smile and fair exterior, that when it would destroy you seems a very paradox of honesty. You, good and loyal reader, have cast your lines in happier places than have fallen to the lot of thousands of your fellow Americans; for, although in New York and Philadelphia, and Boston and Cincinnati, and even in such cities as Portland, Springfield, Albany, Brooklyn, Indianapolis and Detroit, there are feeble organizations of the Knights, a wholesome public sentiment has kept them in tolerable subjection.

"But, MEN OF THE NORTH, be vigilant, watchful as the angels of the night that guard you when devils plot and plod through darkness and light. From many, many woes and tortures—tortures that emaciate the body, unsettle the mind and damn the soul to eternal agony—I would save you!

"Can it be possible that any one who, having mind enough to comprehend the smallest things of earth, will deny that there exists a horrid complot, a foul conspiracy that strikes at the very roots of our liberties, that seeks to rudely tear asunder the glorious legacy of a united brotherhood of States, that was signed and sealed with the best blood of our noble forefathers; that labors untiringly to disrupt our county and tear in twain our nation?

"Who will deny this?

"Do we not each day, as time speeds on, hear the morning gun and the evening gun of the enemy on our borders? Do we not from every battlefield hear of tortures and wounds of our sons and brothers, and those who are dear to us? And the great record of the heroic dead! On fame's imperishable tablets, the myriads of names that stand out in letters of light, of those who freely gave their lives an offering to liberty, prove that an effort of the most fiendish desperation, on a scale of hellish magnificence unprecedented in the history of the world, has been made by the leaders of the secession movement, to undermine and overthrow, at all hazards, the Union and the Constitution.

"Who will deny this?

"Who? Why the Knight and the Copperhead—*arcades ambo!* They are those who are the friends of the Union (*as they want it*), and the Constitution (*as it never was and never will be*). The Knights of the Golden Circle are the fathers and mothers of Secession, and the Copperheads are their weak and sickly bantlings. They would not attack the Union nor injure the Constitution! Oh, no! not they! Like Judas, they would betray with a kiss; and like Brutus, stab you to the heart while smiling in simulated friendship! They are not bound by any compact, except with members of their own order, and all their oaths, and bonds and protestations to others, are made without faith!

"Who is the foe that to-day flaunts a strange banner in our faces, as the emblem of a separate nationality in our young Republic? Whose serried ranks menace our homes, and threaten to make them the scene of a bloody conflict? Do we know this enemy? Is he merely the Southerner, who thinks his rights are assailed, and who fears an abridgment of some of his esteemed privileges? Is it the disciple of the true democracy, who takes a bold stand for the rule of the people?

"No, no, none of these!

"On the red field of Antietam, there was an officer of exalted rank in the Southern army, whose hair of silvery grey gave dignity to his appearance, and whose counsels commanded the respect of his companions in arms. Among the marks of his rank, there sparkled a strange jewel, a golden serpent coiled in a circle, and crested with jet enamel. The eyes of the serpent were formed of beautiful diamonds, that fired and sparkled with every movement, of the wearer. The ornament conveys no riddle. The darkness of the night is black to our sense of seeing; so was the crest of the serpent. The coil was a golden circle. What more simple? Knight of the Golden Circle! But why the emblematic serpent?

"In the midst of the bloody slaughter of that bravely contested field, the man of the silvery locks and serpent emblem, led a division to charge the center of the Union army. He rode madly, and wildly urged his men to the fray; but a movment on the part of the Northern troops to flank his command had escaped his attention, till he found himself hemmed in with only two regiments to second his efforts, the balance of the division engaged against great odds, and his situation was desperate in the extreme. At that moment, a new rallying cry from their foes, greeted the ears of the Union boys. 'Red Rose! Red Rose! to the rescue!'" Mark the result: The fire on the Southerners almost entirely ceased, and a

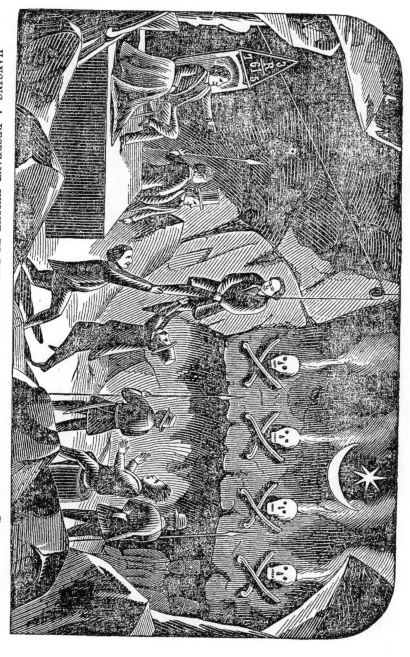

HANGING A RECREANT KNIGHT IN THE DUNGEON OF AN ARKANSAS CASTLE—See page 33.

2

General with two regiments, that were justly prisoners to the skill and prowess of the Union arms, marched away to rejoin their division, with little more trouble than they would have had in the ordinary evolutions of a dress parade! The Red Rose is not peculiar, then, to the Southern clime. It blooms also at the North, and was represented in both armies at Antietam!

"In the Union Army there was a regiment known as 'One Hundred and Ninth Illinois.' Where is it, and what is its record? It was raised in that gloriously loyal and truly patriotic State, nominally in response to the call of our Government for men to fight the battles of the Union; but ye who doubt the power and influence, and intentions, and damnable purposes of the Legion of the Circle, mark the result! Every man of that regiment, from its colonel to the extreme tattered end of its last hanger-on, was connected with lodges, temples, or hives of the Knights; and after betraying into the hands of our foes full details of all our plans, and assisting them to rob us of large amounts of property, they went over, every man,—body, soul, and breeches,—to the army of the Secessionists! Innumerable facts, of the same general character, are patent to the world.

"Who conveys, in untranslatable cipher, or cunningly-devised hieroglyphics, information to our Southern foe of all our plans and movements? We can not and must not shut our eyes to the humiliating fact that they receive such information daily; but how do they get it? Spies sent from the South? Never! A thousand Southern spies could not effect, for the cause of Secession, what is now done for it, by those in sympathy with its foul purposes in our very midst.

The serpent with the glittering eyes has coiled its slimy folds around weak men and bad men, at the North, and is dragging them away, unceasingly, to its great prototype and master, the devil. The serpent with the glittering eyes is the king of the Copperheads! They bow down to him, and do his bidding; and grow weary with "watching over the border," that he may profit thereby.

"Men of the North, beware of the serpent!

"What is the record of REUBEN STOUT, a member of the Sixtieth Indiana Infantry? He, poor boy, was shot at Johnson's Island, in October last (1863) for desertion; but, before his death, he made a confession. He was allowed to go home on furlough, and when there, he states with his dying breath, he was met by several Copperheads, who persuaded him not to return, and promised him protection. They told him that it was a vile ' Abolition war,' for the benefit of the negro against the white man, or for negro equality. That the man who would fight in such a cause, lowered himself below the grade of the African. They induced him to join the Knights of the Golden Circle, and he states that one of the obligations of the order bound him to do all he could against the war, — to resist the draft, if one should be made ; and likewise to resist and . oppose all confiscation and emancipation measures, in every possible way. The members were also sworn to stand by each other in all measures of resistance, and to do all they could to prevent another man or dollar going from the State for the further prosecution of the war. This was the lesson that men, who should have had discretion, taught this inexperienced boy ; and, acting in accordance with such teachings, when a squad attempted to arrest him, he killed one of the party. Compared with those Indiana Copperheads, he was guiltless ; and they should have suffered the punishment. If the devil does not get them, there is little use of having a devil any longer !

" Of course, these references to individual cases will be understood as simply in elucidation of general facts. Incidents of the same character might be recited to the extent of an ordinary volume, and even then leave the story incomplete. Still these facts are not appreciated. There is an undefined impression or slow belief in the minds of a majority of the people that there is something wrong in the management of things ; that there is a bad leak somewhere, but they are above believing in a conspiracy at the North, to play into the hands of the enemy. The plain, unvarnished facts are understood by but few, but with that few there is no mistake.

" Mark it !

" There is a powerful secession organization at the North, growing daily more powerful, and using every means at their command for the success of the so-called Confederates. We may call them Copperheads, Knights of the Golden Circle, Butternuts, or whatever else we please, the facts lead to the same aggregate result, and the names are sufficiently synonymous to be included under one general classification.

"Mark it again, men of the North!

"Not to leave any one in the dark regarding this writing, I have been for years a member of the Order of Knights. I knew the organization in its infancy, when the Secession of the Southern States was only hinted at in whispers among a chosen few; when not more than sixty men in the whole land knew there was such a purpose in the mind of anybody; and when, in all the cotton states but one, such an idea would have been scouted as the rankest treason. It is no freak of these latter days. It is older than South Carolina nullification, for that was the still-born offspring of its epileptic conception. Since that time, it has daily grown in strength and stature, spreading its, branches far and wide, until it has made its power felt in nearly every State of America. It is a powerful Order, and the danger lies in the fact that its power is vastly underrated by the unitiated.

"I have sufficient reason to know what its power is. I have seen it exercised in more ways than I have inclination to recite. I have known it to part husband and wife, parent and child, brother and sister, to tear asunder the bonds of the church, to murder the weak, and drive the indigent forth to starve! I have seen it rob virtue of its brightest jewels, and murder chastity in sportive glee! The blood of its victims, sacrificed for opinion's sake, would float an argosy; and, altogether, the history of its crimes form a record so damning that it would disgust and appal a thousand generations of Neros and Borgias! It has tracked me thousands of miles— twice across the Atlantic, once beyond the Rocky Mountains, over half the States of the North, and its bloodhounds are to-day on my track, I have no doubt.

"Less than a week ago, I recognized a peculiar sign made by a gentleman in the streets of the city where I am now writing. I answered it instinctively, without thought. He came close to me, and spoke as follows:

"Up Court 3. *On the white.*"

"I bowed, and passed on. I walked slowly till I came to a corner of the square, and then I didn't walk slowly. I made all haste to my boarding-house, and changed my clothes completely, disguising myself in clothing I had procured for the purpose against a time of

need.   My informant had told me, in the above apparently-senseless
message, that there was to be an immediate meeting of the Court
Street Hive, for the reason that there was a Southern traitor among
us.   Too well I knew who that traitor was, and what the action of
the meeting would be could they catch him.   My life would not
be worth praying for ; but they were not shrewd in the selection of
a messenger to carry the summons, and so I have again escaped.
O my God ! how long shall such things prosper in a free country ?

CHAPTER II.

Renewal of Old Acquaintance—Who propagates the Mongrel Breed of Yellow Pine-colored Wenches and Mahogany Male Chattels—There are True Men North and South—Gin and Sugar an Infallible Remedy for Yankee Bloodletting of Southern Chivalry—The Author talks like a Plymouth Rock Boy—Scripture will not do for Slaves—A Yankee Wife Charms the Ire of a Veteran Knight.

IT was pleasant to be at home again, and I was disposed to enjoy life to the utmost; for I was blessed with a jewel of a wife, good health, and a cheerful disposition. I remained very much secluded for several days in the enjoyment of home scenes and domestic comfort; but, by degrees, I began to mingle again with old acquaintances, and to attempt the renewal of former friendships. Old acquaintances, however, were shy, and did not exhibit the cordiality of former years. They stood aloof and let me do most of the talking. All at once it occurred to me that they were watching my expressions very closely, and I therefore made an attempt to place my mouth under guard; but an occasional expression of admiration for something I had seen, heard or read about, at the North, would escape me in spite of all my precautions, and it soon leaked out, through some information conveyed to my mother, that I was "spotted," *i. e.*, tinctured with Abolition sentiments. Of course, I denied such a charge as I would any base slander, and embraced every convenient occasion to stamp it with falsehood.

Among the few interrogatories put to me by my quondam but now distant friends, I was asked if Northern men were not generally wedded with negresses; and when I assured them that such was not the case, I was met by that class of looks that certain people put on when they doubt your statements.

"Whar, then," queried one of my interrogators, "is all your amalgermationists?"

"I fear, sir," was my rejoinder, "that they exist *practically* only at the South."

" That's another d—d Abolition lie you have heard from the Yankees," he screamed, in great rage.

In one moment I saw the blood flying from his nose, and he was bellowing like a mad bull. In another moment I heard the report of a pistol, my cap flew from my head, and a pistol ball traversed the crest of my *caput*, tearing the hair away, and raising an ugly welt as large as my finger. My first impression was that my head had gone with the cap, and actually looked around to see if such were the case; but about that time there came a startling cry that I shall never forget. The maddened crowd had become perfectly infuriated, and they raised the shout of " Hang the Abolitionist! Hang the d—d Yankee spy !"

Had I acted on my first impulse, I would have made an inglorious retreat, but a second thought decided me to stand my ground, let the consequences be what they might. I mounted a cotton bale and waited. Soon as a few men were near enough, I said I wished to speak a few words before they proceeded further, and from what I knew of them, I felt sure they would not deny me a hearing. The compliment was rather graciously received, and it was intimated that I might proceed.

" Now, boys," said I, " you all know that I have just returned from a long visit to the North, where I have enjoyed myself pretty well, for it was my first visit there, and I have seen many new things. I have learned facts that are worth knowing, many of which I would not have believed had I not seen them. I found in that cold land a degree of energy and unselfish enlightenment that stamps its people with the signet of a higher nobility than rank or wealth. A frugal yet hospitable people; saving, yet generous; not rich, yet liberal with what they have. A calm, deliberate people; if intense and warm in any one thing, it is an ardent and sincere love of country—revering the memory of WASHINGTON— respecting the Constitution and the Rights of Man. A people sincere in their dealings, always carefully observing the golden rule. A sympathetic race, of generous impulses; sustaining large benevolent institutions; where the offspring of the unfortunate are provided for, and taught the rudiments of an English education. These things all struck me as new, and deserving of credit. I did not expect to find them, and was so agreeably disappointed and favorably impressed, that I felt bound to do justice to a people that we have not properly understood. But if you think I have sur-

THE ANTE-ROOM OF THE SERPENT—See page 43.

rendered one iota of my devotion to State rights, or the institutions of the South, you are mistaken in the man. (Cheers.) I was born here, and here is my home. Here live my parents, and here is my fortune. Let us all, however, reserve the right of respecting TRUE MEN wherever we may find them."

The crowd added another instance to the instability of popular sentiment, by greeting the conclusion of this harangue with hearty cheers, and it was at once voted that I should shake hands and make it up all around. Nobody was backward at this except the gentleman my fist had wounded about the nose, and he very quietly subsided when it was discovered that the "make up" was composed of a liberal admixture of gin and sugar. As we were drinking, my father joined the party, and I saw him passing busily from one to another, in earnest conversation. After a time he came and took me by the hand.

"Well, my boy," said he, "they tell me you have had a little brush and came out top; in fact, that you did the gentlemanly thing altogether, and floored the party. The sentiments you expressed about the Northerners are all wrong, though. You didn't see but few, of the better class, and didn't get much acquainted with them. But come, the boys will excuse you now, and I want to see you at home, where we can talk more at leisure."

As we passed through the entrance hall, I met my wife, and thought I detected the traces of tears on her cheek. I was about to inquire the cause of her grief, when my father again urged his request for an immediate interview. I therefore repressed my feelings for the moment, and went with him. To my surprise, he conducted me to an unused room in the attic, and, after we were seated, addressed me substantially in these words:

"You have always been a source of pride and satisfaction to me, my son. You have never been guilty of an act that has given me real pain, until you married a Yankee wife. I wonder why you did so, and am sorry that you did not advise with me first. But that is done, and can't be helped now, that I see. I am anxious that you occupy the position your station in life entitles you to, and, having that end in view, I have proposed you for admittance into one of the best and most honorable societies that ever existed. It is composed of our best men, and none others can ever become members."

"I am sure," I replied, "that I feel very much complimented by this attention, and hope I shall prove deserving. But what is the object of the Society?"

"The protection of our rights,—the security of our property, and our station in society."

"But what rights have we more than other men, that need protection?"

"All of our rights, my boy, as Southern gentlemen, are more or less in danger."

"From what?"

"Well, to come directly to the point, from the encroachments of the North. I suppose you will feel like combating this point, to some extent, but don't waste your breath on me. I know whereof I speak, and at the proper time you will see as I do. I am so much your senior in years, and your natural guardian, that it were not best for us to differ in opinion on a point where we will soon be forced to agree. There will be a meeting of the Society to-night, and I wish you to go."

"Most certainly I will go, out of respect to your wishes, if with no other motive. But I am truly grieved, sir, that you do not approve of my choice of a wife, and hope you will soon see cause to change your views. I look upon Lucy as a model of her sex, and you will share in my admiration, when you come to know her better."

"No, Edward, I shall never like an Abolitionist, under any circumstances."

"Well, there I am with you, neck and neck," I replied, jocosely; "but Lucy is no more an Abolitionist than yourself."

"Tut! tut! All Yankees are Abolitionists and nigger thieves; and 'tain't two hours ago that I had to scold your darling for trying to beat some Scripture verses into little nigs' heads. A devil of a time we would have with them, if they were to get a little Scripture learning!"

"What did you say to Lucy, father?"

"Why, when I saw what she was at, I was mad, and told her I reckoned you didn't bring her here to run wild with the little nigs; but, if you did, that she should have a canvass frock in welcome, for I reckoned she wouldn't disgrace it. Now don't rile up so, Ed.; recollect I was mad, and couldn't help it."

"Father, my wife is a lady, and you are a gentleman. The first part of this proposition we all understand well enough, but I fear *she* has some doubt of the integrant. Now let me ask what you would do if a gentleman should speak thus to mother?"

"But, Ned, no gentleman would do— Eh? what was I saying? Well, 'pon my word. I think somebody has made an ass of my— my—*him*self, I should say. Let's go down and find the girl, Ned, and you apologize for me, there's a good boy."

"Apologize for you, my father? No, not I. If an apology is necessary, I don't think she will receive it from me, and perhaps not from you."

"What, not from me? She won't fight, I reckon, so it's apology or nothing. You go and speak to her first, Ned."

As we reached the hall, I heard Lucy at the piano, and therefore led my father into the parlor. Tapping her on the shoulder to stop the music, I said:

"Here is a gentleman, Lucy, that has changed his mind on the question of the canvas frock, and waits to tell you so."

"Eh, eh? Ned! Now, that't too bad. Who said I had changed my mind?"

"I know you have *not*," said my wife, "for you did not speak your mind when you made that funny speech. No gentleman ever used such words, meaning them, and I am sure, my dear father, if there ever was a perfect gentleman, you are the one," and before he could divine her intention, she threw her arms around his neck and saluted him with a burning kiss.

That and the "perfect gentleman" idea did the work completely. The expression on my father's face, as Lucy released him, was worth living many years to see. It was unlike anything I ever witnessed, and I knew there was a holy compact of love and faith between those two persons from that moment. The old man couldn't find words for some minutes, but finally he stammered out,

"She aint no nig—eh?—Abolitionist, I mean, after all, is she, Ned?" and ran out of the room like an abashed schoolboy.

"What a dear, kind, good old man," said Lucy. She would hear no explanations nor apologies from me, and looked upon the matter as entirely settled, without my intervention.

CHAPTER III.

QUALIFICATIONS for Knighthood—Aristocracy the Standard—Initiation—Satanic
Oath—Awful Scene in an Alabama Temple—How the Order Raises the
Financial Sinews of War—The "Gray Cross "—The "Raven's Plume "—
"Master of the Rose of the Circle"—Location of Lodges in Northern States—
"Trust not a Coward where the Wind blows cold."

ACCOMPANIED by my father and several neighbors, I set out soon
after dark in the evening of the day in which the events related in
the previous chapter occurred, to attend my first meeting with the
Knights of the Golden Circle. At that time, I knew as little of the
character of this organization, and its real objects, as an unborn
child; and, therefore, the conversation between my father and his
friends, was like an unknown tongue to me. I had not learned, at
that time, that words were mere arbitrary sounds, and that "black
could be used to describe any other color just as well as the real
name of the other color, provided the signification of the word had
been previously changed by agreement. But I have since found
that it is extremely easy, especially with Knights of the Golden
Circle, to say one thing and mean another! The peculiarity of the
language they speak among themselves, would require a volume as
large as Webster's Unabridged to fully explain, while the peculiar
meaning they give to the words of our language, would drive all
the lexicographers crazy.

When we arrived at the place of rendezvous, I was introduced
into a splendidly furnished apartment, where I found three or four
gentlemen seated in anxious expectation of something they didn't
seem to know whether they wanted or not, and was told this was
the retiring room for candidates that were awaiting initiation. It
was a comfortable place to lounge, and I was fully content, especially
as I found the other gentlemen were intelligent and disposed to
converse.

As their conversation, however, will possess no interest at this
time for the general reader, I will not transcribe it, but give instead

the important points of the initiation service of the Knights, as I learned them on this occasion.

The person proposed for membership must be of legal age. If an old man, must be vouched for, as a pro-slavery Democrat with a straight record. If he is only of age, he must be known and recommended as favoring the extension of slavery by every means at his command. All candidates must be men of wealth, and, if living South, slaveholders; therefore, a cardinal principle is to establish and maintain an aristocracy.

It having been ascertained, upon examination, that he possesses the requisite qualifications, the candidate is conducted by the Pilgrim to the Sentry on guard. He, speaking in a smothered tone, inquires,

" Who goes there ?"

Answer : " A friend to the cause."

Question : " What do you seek ?"

Answer : " Admission to the temple."

Question : " Where does it lie ?"

Answer : " In the innermost secret chamber of the castle."

Question : " How speeds the night ?"

Answer : " It is well."

To which the Sentry responds :

" Advance, then, and receive the oath of silence and secrecy."

The figure 7 is then exhibited, which, translated, means : " The draw-bridge is down."

The Pilgrim then enters, and passes through the ante-room into the castle, leaving the candidate in charge of the Keeper of the Gates of the castle, who places upon his (the candidate's) head a cap, the front of which extends down over the face, and shuts out everything from his sight. After this is accomplished, the Pilgrim returns, in company with the Provost, who, with great (apparent) difficulty, passes the candidate through the gate.

When they arrive at the inner door of the ante-room, the Provost strikes his sword against it, and it is immediately opened. Within a file of six men appear, two of whom bear strangely-fashioned lamps, formed of human skulls, and painted with fantastic shapes, that are thrown out in weird relief by the light within ; two hold heavy broadswords, with cabalistic inscriptions and strange devices, and two with skull and cross-bones upon a blood-stained cloth, fill up the measure of the poor devil's shivering agony. The vizor is then lifted, and the affrighted gaze of the novice fastens on a scene that freezes the blood in his veins. He had never imagined that hell itself could produce a spectacle so revolting to the finer feelings of man's nature; and for some temperaments, the fright of that moment is the nightmare of a lifetime.

The Provost then addresses the candidate :

" You seek admission to the secrets of a cause which will make your name, in ages yet to come, glorious in the bright page whereon the faithful historian records renowned men and famous deeds. Should you betray its trust to them we hate, *a fate more terrible than death itself awaits you!* We visit revenge upon the weak, and upon those who are innocent of your dread crime. All whom you love—*your wife, your sister, your child, your aged mother*, and everything on earth you call your own, all, all is forever lost to you if you breathe to mortal ear one word, or letter, or sign of the secrets we confide in you. Nay, more. If you ever write, or print, or engrave, or in any manner impart the least shadow of a hint regarding the secret signs, symbols, or purposes of this Order, your punishment shall task all the ingenuity of diabolical torture, to expiate your horrible crime. Forever hopeless, cheerless WHILE YOU LIVE, will be your lot on earth—a starving miscreant, beggar, praying for death through years of torture! You can not, dare not, shall not recede. From this time onward, we own and hold your very life! You know the history of the Italian Carbonari. If you do not, neglect no opportunity to read it, until you know what tortures are meet for those who betray great trusts. Blood has been shed ere now in the dungeous of our castles, and it shall again before our work is done. Lives have been sacrificed, and they who speak against us, whether within or without our temples, shall perish like dogs, and the flesh of their bones become the food of buzzards and vultures!

" Both friend and foe alike shall find,
" We keep our compact with mankind.
" By shot and shell,
" By sword and flame,
" By draughts from hell,
" We 'll keep our fame !
" Whoever dares our cause reveal,
" Shall test the strength of knightly steel ;
" And when the torture proves too dull,

A "KNIGHTLY" ATTACK ON A UNIONIST—See page 59.

" We 'll scrape the brains from out his skull,
" And place a lamp within the shell,
" To light his soul from here to hell.
" What, ho ! a craven ! (Spoken in a very loud and startling tone.) Cut him down, my men, with your good broadswords, and let the milk from his veins—we want no cowards."

The swordsmen raise their weapons aloft, and then comes the test of nerve. If the candidate wavers, or appears frightened, he is pricked unmercifully, occasionally drawing blood—and instances are known where the novice has been maimed for life, while his tortures were enjoyed at this rare sport !

After this amusing by-play has lasted till the worthy Knights are satisfied, the candidate is handcuffed and gagged, his legs being left free, and conducted to the large hall known as the *Knight's Temple*, where every person present wears a helmet, with the vizor drawn over his features. As he is passed slowly by the Knights, attended by the Provost and six guards (who are known as Plebians), each Knight repeats, calling the candidate's name :

" I know thee ; break not thine oath ! "

.This part of the ceremony is very impressive, when properly conducted, and is very apt to set a man of sense to thinking. He begins to wonder, at about this time, if he hasn't wondered before, what all this mummery means, and feels that he wishes himself out of the scrape. The mist, however, comes at an unlucky moment, for at this point his vizor is removed, and the representation of a scene such as he never will forget, never can forget, meets his bewildered gaze. The machinery, figures, and all the surroundings, are so perfect, it looks like an actual transaction, representing the death by hanging of a frightened candidate, who, having reached this point of the service, after several severe broadsword cuts and horrible bruises, refuses to proceed. The occurrence was real, and disgraces the annals of a temple in Alabama, in the dungeon of which the poor, helpless wretch was pulled up by a rope drawn over a pulley, while two hardened villains tugged up his legs, till the life was choked out of him. How many times since the same thing has actually occurred, I am unable to state ; but Knights have, on several occasions within my own knowledge, courted opportunities to re-enact the horrid murder ; and have assured me that nothing would give them more pleasure than to assist at such an execution ! (*See cut.*)

The candidate now understands why his arms were pinioned, his mouth gagged, and his legs left free. The scene is fully explained to him, and all its devilish details dwelt upon with a gusto that devils might relish. The scene from which the sketch was made, illustrating the above statement, is in general use throughout the "Bivouac" of the Southern States, and especially is this true in Georgia, Florida, Alabama, and North and South Carolina. As the novice gazes upon the fearful scene, the Knights slowly repeat, in unison:

"Beware, or such shall be thy doom!"

This is repeated three times, each time more solemnly than the preceding. On either side of him stand the two guards, bearing the skulls and cross-bones on a blood-stained cloth, continually moving them in the most favorable positions to attract his attention and making a display of a disgustingly nauseating character.

These emblems are figurative; the skulls representing death to Abolitionists, and the cross-bones death to traitors.

Before the candidate, stand the two guards with drawn swords, and behind them is represented a piratical looking ship, typical of the slave trade. One of the Knights bears a crescent, which is intended to symbolize "A Growing South," and its wearer is known as the Grand Knight, by those who have taken only the initiatory degree of the order. After the lesson of the Alabama murder scene has been properly impressed upon the mind of the candidate, he is led rapidly three times around the room, followed closely by several Knights, and halted at the chair of the Crescent. The Grand Knight then addresses him in these words:

"Sir novice, I perceive that you have been selected by our oath bound brotherhood for the performance of a great and noble duty; but, in accordance with our rites, it is necessary that you join us and become firmly united in our cause. Are you willing to subscribe to our oath and conform to our customs?" (It matters little to the Knights whether the candidate is willing or not.) "After entering this temple, you can only depart from it a member of our order, or a corpse."

The candidate, trembling with fear, is then bound in irons, placed upon his knees, and compelled to repeat the following oath; (the gag having been removed); while two "Post Captains of Ordnance" stand with pistols aimed at his head:

FORM OF OATH.

"I, (giving full name), do hereby most solemnly declare and protest, without any mental reservation whatever, that while living, I will give my heartiest co-operation, my energies, my talents and my property to the cause of this order, *be that cause whatever it may.* That it shall be my duty, from which I will never retire, to sustain and cherish the institutions of the South against all adversaries. That in war, as in peace, I will cheerfully obey the Chief, and all subordinate commanders, of this or any other Temple, that may call my services into requisition. I do furthermore swear that I will never hold friendship with any one, save the slave dealer and owner; that I believe the poor whites in our midst are the enemies of our institutions, and can not be trusted; and that the sooner they are reduced to the condition of serfs, the safer will be our government and property. I do furthermore swear to bear hatred, that nothing but blood shall satisfy, against all men of the North who are not friendly to our cause. I also most solemnly declare to you, O, Knights of Power, and, here upon my bended knees, I swear by my soul, and by the God who made it, that, should the " Stars of the South " ever separate from the North, I will at once hold myself in readiness to march forth with you to do battle against the Northern foe. I furthermore swear to sow the seeds of hatred and revenge against the Northern States, among all the men of the South, with whom I come in contact; and to stir up dissensions and quarrels among Northern men, whenever I have opportunity. This do I further declare, that I will ever prove faithful and true to my fellow craftsmen; that I will never betray to living man what I have seen to-night, what I have heard, nor whatsoever I shall hereafter see or hear. Binding myself hereunto, without redress, to suffer any penalty this or any other Temple may choose to inflict, if I in any degree infract the letter, meaning, or any shadow of the intent of this my solemn obligation. This is my oath."

To which all the Knights assembled respond, " It is his oath.'

This is spoken three times slowly and solemnly, and between each repetition a large bell sounds a muffled toll. After which all exclaim, as with one voice:

"Hear and record it."

After signing the Compact, which embraces the Constitution and By-Laws of the Order, and in which is incorporated the substance of the oath, the candidate is instructed in the various ways of entering a lodge. As these forms are constantly changing, for several reasons that seem sufficient to warrant a change, and as they were always somewhat different in different localities, I will not enter into details regarding them."

The initiation fee in the Castle where I was admitted, was fifty dollars, beside a tax of two and a half per cent on the total valuation of the candidates' effects, which tax he was allowed to pay in twelve monthly installments. The tax assessed against candidates at our Castle in a single night, amounted to $9,240; and in some Castles, it has very much exceeded this sum at a single meeting; so the question of where the money comes from, to carry on the operations of such an organization, is very easily answered. The fund it accumulated before the breaking out of the rebellion, furnished "the sinews of war" for many a desperate scheme, that otherwise would have existed only in the theoretical brain of some desperate secessionist.

After I had passed through the entire programme of the initiatory degree, paid my fees, and pocketed the notice of assessments against my effects, I was coolly informed by the G. K. that I was as yet no Knight; that this ceremony was merely conditional, and only fitted me to receive the degrees of a true Knight at a subsequent period! That my station in society would enable me to exert a commanding influence in favor of the order, and it was therefore expected of me to name an early date for a full insight. I replied that I would consider the matter before naming the time, and soon inform him of my determination. Without seeming to notice my remark, he called the Knights to order, and made the following announcements:

"We will *all* meet here this day week to confer upon Edmund Wright the degree of T. F. 18. Every Knight must be punctual and vigilant. The guards will conduct our friend to the ante-room, as he is not yet entitled to be present at the ceremony of closing."

I was immediately hurried away, with a protest half-formed to utter against this summary disposition of my free agency, but it was just as well I did not speak my mind, for I have since ascertained how useless it would have been. A novice in the order is not allowed to have any will, and a full-grown Knight is in little better position.

It does not seem necessary for me to describe in detail the several degrees of this infamous league; but, for the purposes of this narrative, will content myself by explaining whatever technicalities I may find it necessary to use, at the time I employ them. The candidate passes through several gradations before he begins to fairly understand the true character and the true purposes of the Knights of the Circle. His situation in life may deter him from reaching the highest degrees. Few ever go farther than the " Grey Cross," the meaning of which is, the owner of slaves and favorable to the project of enslaving the poorer whites. If he reaches the " Raven's Plume," he is made a member of the navy, for " Raven's Plume," in the mystic vocabulary of the Knights, signifies the winds of the ocean. If he progresses far enough, he becomes " Master of the Rose of the Circle," which last baptism is interpreted: Circle, i. e., veins; rose, i. e., blood; a blood-letter, which signifies that he may hold rank in the army.

Very few attain to this latter position—only the sons of the most aristocratic and wealthy enjoy the high privilege.

There is no mistake that from the very beginning the Knights of the Golden Circle were intended to be represented only by the rich, for, in the Cotton States, the rich man only has influence and character; but, at the North, the man of moderate means, in many cases, enjoys a social position that commands the highest respect; and therefore, regarding the question of wealth, the Copperhead requirements are modified in the Free States.

According to the original programme, each State possessed a Grand Castle; at least this was the intention of the founders of the order; but for the whole six New England States there never was instituted but one lodge, the rendezvous of which was a dilapidated building, I think in Milk street. New York had nine—four in the country and five in the city. Pennsylvania had five—three in Philadelphia, on Chestnut, Callowhill and Eleventh streets; one at Pittsburgh, and one in the Lehigh Valley, I believe at Mauch Chunk. Ohio had three—one at Cincinnati, one at Dayton, and one at Columbus. Indiana had one at Indianapolis, one at Madison, and one at New Albany. Illinois—two at Chicago, and one at Cairo.

So much for the Northern States in 1858; while in every Southern State Castles were being opened in every direction, and the greatest industry was manifest in making proselytes to the doctrines of the order.

The Castles at the North were not as ably conducted as those at the South, nor entirely on the same plan. The ritual and forms of initiation for the North, although framed on the basis of the original, as used at the institution of the order, were essentially changed. The Northern Castles were principally organized by Southerners, however, although they did not think it expedient to trust their cooler-blooded brethren with their full secrets; for in the White Book of the Seventh Degree appears a "White Plume," which means, in the fourth interpretation, "Trust not a coward when the wind blows cold." Which idea clearly signifies, and was so understood, that the Southerner has ever held the prowess of the men of the North in poor esteem. Some of them have recently had occasion to change their estimate of Yankee valor.

HORRIBLE DEATH OF LITTLE JACK.—See page 65.

CHAPTER IV.

ADHERENCE to the Order, or Death—The South, Right or Wrong—Sectional Prejudices—The Test Oath—Illusions—The Author Astounded, but not Cowarded—The Flaming Serpent—The Final Oath—The Mission of Man, White or Black—The Fiend-like Group—Knight of the "Columbian Star" —Sir Ass—Blasphemy of the K. G.

DURING the week that intervened between my introduction to the Castle, and the time appointed to put me through another course, I felt

> " Like him that shoots up high, looks for the shaft,
> And finds it in his forehead."

I felt guilty of some undefined enormity that would end in shame; and so thoroughly was I convinced that facts would not belie my forebodings, I sought my father and expressed my desire to proceed no farther with the Knights. The old gentleman was greatly troubled, and said to me :

"You will feel differently after you have really taken a degree that has something in it. And then it is not possible for you to retract now; it will not be allowed."

" But who will prevent me, if I am so disposed ?"

" Everybody that you saw at the Castle, Ned, will prevent you, myself included. There is no other course for us but to go ahead, and you must go, too."

" If I refuse, what then ?"

" To tell you the truth, my son, I hardly think you could persist in refusing, *and live.* A man over on Salt Creek refused to take the initiatory, after several warnings. He was finally notified that he must join without further ceremony; but he sent word he would see them all d——d first. In less than a week that man disappeared, and has not since been seen, although his family has spent time and money to discover him. It was positively announced at our Castle, three weeks ago, *that he would never be seen again on earth,* and we know that such announcements are strictly true !"

"But, father, you do not approve of such things? It can not be!"

"Well, I don't know. Things have come to a strange issue. We must protect ourselves and our property; and those who will not help us will help our enemies. This is the way we are forced to reason the matter, and every true Southern Rights' man will join the Knights without trouble. Those that will not join, we know are not true to our cause."

"Of course you do not doubt my fidelity to the South, and still I feel a strange reluctance to proceed in this matter."

"You must overcome your reluctance, for it is necessary that we all work in unison; and, although some things may appear strange to you, and some minor particulars absolutely wrong, I hold it is our bounden duty to ourselves and the glorious cause of our loved South, to form a close and invincible compact for the utter destruction of our enemies. You must compromise with your objecting, and become convinced of what you will soon know to be the fact, that our cause is the cause of right and of justice, approved of God and our consciences."

Poor, infatuated old man! how bitterly was he deceived!

I saw the uselessness of further argument and the hopelessness of my position, in making an effort to suspend further progress with the Knights; for the league in which my father had so strong a faith, and of whose power he had given me such horrible proof, would doubtless compel my presence and participation in their ceremonies, *nolens volens*. I therefore replied:

"Probably I have let imagination interfere too much with reason, for I am satisfied that you, my father, would not join, nor counsel your son to league himself with, anything dishonorable. I will therefore waive objections to the order, till I see more reason for them."

"A wise decision, Ned; and I congratulate you thereon. We must act together, and in union with our friends, or our cause is lost. Everything for the South is our motto."

I will not disguise the fact that to a great extent I participated in the general enthusiasm for the South, and persuaded myself that the feeling was genuine patriotism. Such is the error into which thousands of better men at the South have carelessly fallen; and the rock on which thousands of fanatics, in all parts of our land, have sought to founder the Union. Sectional prejudice was at first excited by the unholy ambition of a few unscrupulous leaders in the Cotton States, who pointed to the action of crazy Abolitionists as expressive of the sentiments of the Northern people; and it was generally believed at the South, even at the time of which I write, that Northerner and Abolitionist were synonymous classifications. And this feeling the Southern people persuaded themselves, was genuine love of country, instead of carefully sifting the facts, in which event they would have made the discovery that it was only sectional prejudice, the unreasoning enemy of all good, the destroyer of peace and arch-fiend of discord! But I did not participate as madly in this blind error as those who were without the benefit of observation at the North; and hence my hanging back for the moment.

But it was only for the moment!

When the day arrived in which it was appointed I should take another step toward knighthood, I was firm in my purpose to encounter the fate my friends had predestined. I had smothered all scruples, silenced the qualms of patriotic emotion, and made every effort to believe with my neighbors that the North was our enemy, and took every opportunity to meddle with our institutions and abridge our rights.

I was early at the Castle, but not in advance of any of the members. All seemed to be actuated by an untiring zeal in the service of the Order, and we were soon ready for operations. I was soon waited upon, in the ante-room, by two guides, dressed in robes of crimson velvet, bedizened with silver lace, and bedecked and bespangled with ruby stars and emeralds. The turbans on their heads were of the same material, and ornamented in a similar manner; while their feet were shod in sandals of a strange fashion, and rich with jewels. They wore masks, but so perfectly representing the human face that I did not discover the fact until I saw the same ceremony performed with others, in after initiations; but I was troubled at being waited upon by two strangers, and therefore watched their proceedings with uncomfortable interest.

"Novice," said one, bowing to me, "it becomes our duty before again admitting you to the inner temple, to administer to you, the Test; and it is of the first importance that you faithfully heed its import, and truthfully abide its words. We have all taken it, and it is the pride and boast of every true Knight, that he has been true to its teachings.   You will place your hands on this book, which is the Holy Bible, with us, and we will all repeat, one after the other,

THE TEST OATH.

" We, Novice and Knight, citizens of the South and champions of Southern Rights, do hereby and hereon, in the presence of each other and of Almighty God, Judge of the World, solemnly and sincerely pledge our lives, our faith and honor, to conceal and never expose to mortal being, except to true Knights, who have sworn to this oath, any circumstance or thing that may transpire in this Castle, or in any Castle with which we may be connected ; that we will not disclose the secrets of Knighthood to save life, friend nor· fortune, but that we will freely sacrifice life and everything dear to us if called upon to do so, for the perpetuity of the principles of our glorious order.   That we swear death and destruction to Northern Abolitionists ; and that we will leave no means untried, to circumvent their schemes.   In the name of God.   Amen."

The door of the entrance to the Temple swung open, as we concluded this oath, and I heard the response from all the Knights, as if uttered with one voice :
" In the name of God.   Amen."
Then the door closed and I was thus addressed :
" We have no doubt of your fidelity and honesty of purpose, and if any thing should happen during the ceremony that is now about to commence, that would seem to call you in question or cast a doubt on your intentions, remember that this is the ceremony through which all Knights of our Order have passed ; and we number those among us, that the best and greatest are proud to associate with.   You will now repair to the closet here to the right, where you will find a dress precisely like this of ours, in which you will clothe yourself; and when you have done so, indicate it by three loud and distinct raps within the door."
As I entered the closet I was struck with the strange appearance of all its contents—different from anything I had ever seen, and therefore difficult to describe for want of similes.   One side was covered with an immense tapestry, on which was painted the fabled Sisyphus, tugging away at the eternal rock with Herculean strength,

but ever resultless labor, adjudged to never-ending toil, or instant death from the recoil of the huge mass!

In a curiously-fashioned niche, stood a human skeleton, with arms sustained by some mechanical contrivance, and holding in the bony hands two lamps of grotesque shape that, when I entered, emitted a bright red light, but soon its rays were changed to a green of dazzling intensity, and so remained till I had completed dressing. As, following instructions, I rapped three times within the door, the color of the light changed to a sickly yellow, the tapestry of Sisyphus gently rolled up, as of its own accord, and in the dim vista of what seemed a long and far-off colonade, I saw, as if suspended in mid-air, the circle of the Golden Serpent, bewildering in the brilliancy of burnished metal, and shooting flame from eyes and mouth. It was one of the most cunningly-devised mechanical effects I ever witnessed, and leaves an indelible impression on the mind.

As I looked, I became lost in wonder—forgot where I was, and the object of my mission; in fact, was dreaming, when suddenly the bright serpent seemed to straighten, turn toward me, and extend its enormous fangs; and before I had time to collect my scattered faculties, it made one prodigious leap to strike me! I turned to flee, in the extremity of fear, when I discovered the floor beneath my feet was sinking, the lights were extinguished, and down, down I went, in utter darkness, down continually to a depth that seemed unfathomable, down to the very bowels of the earth, dark and cheerless as the realms of despair! Down, down, down! At last, there was a stop, easy and quiet, but far from satisfactory, for the darkness was oppressive, and the silence utterly desolate.

I sat for a few moments motionless and silent, for some time was required to determine on a course of action, when I exclaimed aloud,

" Well, if this is progression in Knighthood, I've had enough."

Gods! (mythological and earthly) the fright of that moment was almost the death of me! The echo of my words had not died away ere the cavern was illuminated with a hundred brilliant jets! I found myself in the center of a large room, superbly furnished, and occupied by forms of men or devils, attired in the most ridiculous and diabolical disguises, and armed with all sorts of weapons. One, with the form and manner of the Arch Fiend, gave me an unmerciful pricking with his lance, and howled in my ear:

"Ho! ho! and so you're tired of being a Knight, eh? The coward wants to retract!"

With strange unison, and in voices solemn as the death-knell of hope, all the figures responded:

"The coward wants to retract!"

"What shall be done with the black-hearted knave—traitor to his country, and false to his God?" shouted the first speaker.

"Let him suffer the torture, feel the misery of the damned, and die the death of the abandoned miscreant!" responded the united voices of all present.

"Hold, friends!" said I. "No really urgent wish to retract on my part; it was only the desire for more light on what appeared a very dark subject; and when you are ready to proceed, I will be prepared to go ahead—*perge recta via.*"

On the instant, all was darkness again. The mimic devils sat up a dismal howl, that extended into an attenuated wail of such concentrated horror, that all hell seemed to have broken loose! And as the horrid echoes died away in the cavernous depths of the great dungeon, the howl was again taken up, again the wail pierced my ears, and again the echoes ceased their blood-chilling reverberations, only to be repeated in the same fiendish monotonousness! When minutes had been extended into ages by the frightful prolongation of this demoniacal ceremony, and my senses had begun to reel with abject fear, I was startled by a shout, uttered in a voice of thunder close by my ears, and, for months after, sounding in my dreams:

"The serpent! the serpent! Look above you!"

I looked up, and although I knew to a certainty that the effect was produced by mechanical arrangement, that the machinery was moved by my friends and neighbors, and that there was really no fear of bodily harm, I could not, for my life, suppress a great scream of affright as I saw that fiery serpent coiling down toward me, in mid air, lighting his course with bright flame from his mouth and eyes! I made an effort to move, but I had been tied fast without knowing when it was done. I called on my father, and on my neighbors by name; but the only reply was a mocking laugh! O, the sickening agony of that moment! If the damned are subjected to equal torments, every man should make haste to become a Christian.

Down, down, coiled the serpent till I expected the flame he emit-

"CONSCIOUSNESS OF RIGHT AND DUTY TO GOD," AS EXEMPLIFIED IN THE HISTORY OF SOUTHERN KNIGHTHOOD

4

ted would scorch me, and I screamed again and again. Down he came, nearer and nearer; close to my head with a whizzing noise, straitened his huge proportions, and, like a flash, wound himself around my head and neck!

It was more than ordinary manhood could endure : I fainted!

*   *   *   *   *   *   *   *   *

When I was restored to consciousness, I found myself in the great room of the inner Temple, attended by my father and several friends.   Their congratulations were loud, and many were sincere, but I detected some smiles in the crowd of which I did not fancy the complexion ; and it seemed that occasionally when the title of "Knight" was applied to me, it was wrapped in a sneer, and hurled at me derisively.   I afterward learned that these suspicions were substantially correct.

The Grand Knight now approaches, and taking my hand, thus addresses me :

"Brother, I greet thee as a Knight, tried and true ; but in accordance with the usages of this and every other Castle, I have an obligation to administer, that I am sure, after what you have just witnessed and endured, you will not object to.   It has been administered to every one now here present, and all have willingly bound themselves by it.   Are you willing to be similarly bound?"

As I hesitated to promise before knowing the nature of the oath, my father nervously whispered in my ear :

"Say yes, at once, Ned; for God's sake, don't delay.   There is no fooling at this point of the game."

So I said,

"Yes !"

OATH.

"Before God and these witnesses, I, Edmund Wright, a true man, of lawful age and Southern born, do swear that I will never reveal what I have this night witnessed, nor whatever I may hereafter witness in the Castles or Hives of the Knights of the Golden Circle ; that I will keep sacred all the signs, grips, words, and tokens of this order, and never impart them outside of a Castle or Hive, except under urgent necessity, and to those only that I know to be good and true Knights of this degree.   And furthermore, I fully and freely bind myself to each of the following obligations, in perfect good faith, and without the least mental reservation or eva-' sion on my part:

"1st. I swear and promise to conceal the names of the Knights of this degree, the objects and designs thereof, and never, under any circumstances, acknowledge that I am a member, except to such as can give me their sacred word in a manner to leave no doubt that they are true Knights.

"2d. Whatever secrets may be given to me by a Knight of this degree, *no matter what their nature may be*, if imparted as the secret of a knight, and because I am one, I will hold the same sacredly in my own knowledge, and never communicate it, even if my life is at stake. I swear never to speak evil of a brother Knight, but will strive to extenuate his faults, if he have any, and magnify his good qualities on all occasions. I swear never to dishonor the wife or daughter of a Knight, knowing them to be such; but will, on all occasions, consider them under my special protection.

"3d. I swear to oppose, to the utmost of my ability, the admission of any confirmed drunkard, professional gambler, convict, felon, negro, abolitionist, minor, idiot, or foreigner to membership in this degree of the Knights of the Circle; but I will induce as many good Southern Rights' men to join us as possible.

"4th. As interference with the domestic institutions of the South is an enormous crime, condemned by all our laws, I solemnly swear that wherever and whenever I find an abolitionist in a slave State, I will do my utmost to hand him over to the proper authorities, who shall be Knights of this degree, if possible to find them; or, failing to do this, I will kill or maim him to the best of my strength, and the means at my command; so help me God!

"5th. I furthermore solemnly vow and swear that in case a President of the United States is elected, who is not a Southern Rights' man, and from whom any danger to our institutions may be reasonably apprehended, I will do my utmost to destroy his power in the South, even to the taking up of arms against his authority; and in case the Southern States decide to secede from the old Union, I swear to accomplish everything it is in my power to do, to effect this end.

"6th. I do furthermore solemnly swear that I will use my best exertions to discover every man with Northern sympathies in my county, and report the same to this Castle; and I will keep a close watch on all such, and report all suspicious acts on their part at the meetings of this degree. If I learn of any stranger or traveler trading with negroes, or having any communication whatever with them, I swear to inform our Grand Knight at once, that a Council may be convened, and proper steps taken for the punishment of the offender.

"7th. If an insurrection shall occur, and it comes to my knowledge, I will do all I have promised above, or should my own or any other Southern State be invaded by Abolitionists, I will muster the largest force I can, and go to the scene of danger, if well and able to go. I further promise and swear to do all in my power to build up a public sentiment in my State, favorable to the expulsion or enslavement of free negroes; and that no free negro shall marry with my slave, if I can prevent it.

"8th. I furthermore vow and swear that I will report to the Grand Knight the names of all Roman Catholic ministers in my county, as well as all Northern teachers; and no foreigner shall ever receive this degree, one negative vote only being necessary to reject, and in all cases the vote must be taken before the candidate is approached.

"9th. I furthermore swear to exert my influence to reduce the condition of what are known as the "poor whites" with us, to the condition of the negro slave, firmly believing that that condition will subserve his interests, and the interests of the South."

I hesitated at the last clause of the above, and the Grand Knight asked if I had any scruples about proceeding.

"I am sorry to say that I have," was my reply; "for I can not possibly see how the condition of the poor white is to be improved by *reducing* him (your own language) to the condition of the negro slave."

This remark seemed to let loose the pent-up vials of doubt, suspicion of my devotion to the cause, and determination on the part of the Grand Knight to yet more closely enfold me in the toils of the serpent. Darting from his position, with eyes glaring with rage, and his whole countenance distorted, he approached me as if to throttle me.

"Hands off, or by the living God, despite your positon in the Order, I still possess manhood enough to defend myself."

Cowarded by my self-possession, he dropped his uplifted arms and yelled, as only a fiend could:

"Reduce the poor white man to the condition of a slave? Is not his condition already worse than that of our negroes? In the estimation of my slaves, he is but 'poor white trash,' owning nothing and dependent upon his daily labor for a miserable livelihood, while your father, you, and I are lords of the soil, and labor does not, nor should not, sully our higher birthright."

Stung to the quick at his foul scandal upon poor white men, I scornfully replied:

"You, one of the lords of the soil? Why, the poor white man, or even the negro, who tills the soil, and by his labor and enterprise elicits from his mother earth the food that sustains you and me, is filling his mission on that earth, far better, in accordance with the decrees of an overruling Providence, than are they whose idleness tempts them to devise schemes, concocted in hell, to blast the progressive aims of man, be he white or black."

I paused, and astounded at my audacity at having thus given vent to my innate convictions of right, I glanced, timidly in heart, but defiantly in purpose, at the lowering countenance of the Grand Knight, who had stood silently biting his lips while I made the short speech, so annoying to his aristocratic ideas.

Contrary to my expectations, he made no rejoinder; but casting upon me a scowl of malicious contempt, he moved mechanically to a remote part of the room.

Intently watching his motions, I observed him raise his hand and violently jerk a cord, suspended from the ceiling, and almost simultaneously I heard the solemn sound of what might be a muffled bell reverberating along the depths of subterraneous caverns. Immediately a trap-door raised, without any apparent human agency, and from the opened gulf issued a group of moving beings, in appearance unlike any shapes seen on earth or dreamed of as denizens of hell.

The foremost of the fiend-like shapes bore a lantern formed, in the main, of a human skull, surmounted by cross-bones, at the junction of which was a human heart, from which, by some devilish contrivance, blood was flowing, so as partially to obscure the light from that beacon of imagined death to the awe-struck beholder.

Immediately following the lantern-bearer, came another shape (if shape it could be called, that looked unlike any form seen before by mortal eyes), bearing a broad-axe streaming with gore. He was followed by a third, as hideous as the others, and whose insignia of office was a hangman's rope coiled around his misshapen carcase.

In this hellish-looking group, well might I imagine my impending fate.

At the bidding, by sign, of the Grand Knight, the trio advanced to the center of the room, and the Grand Knight hastily confronted me.

"Wavering and irrèsolute man, will you, in spite of the scene now presented to your gaze, falter in your duties to the South, and its most cherished institutions? You are already too far under the influence of our noble and powerful Order to hope for escape. Are you willing to proceed to the attainment of further knowledge in the great mysteries and purposes of the Circle?"

"If the object of the Order be for the benefit of my whole country, South and North, I will advance, under your direction, and take the oaths of obligation as imposed, provided they do not conflict with my honestly-formed convictions of what, as an American citizen, I owe to my fellow-man, let his home be in the South or North."

"North!" yelled the G. K. "Executioners, perform your mission; seize the Yankee Abolitionist. Brothers, approach and witness the just doom of a recreant coward."

On the instant the room became thronged with knights, who rushed from every recess of the murky chamber; for the only light, as I should have stated, came from the skull lantern, barely sufficient to make darkness visible.

"Proceed to the performance of your high commission."

The trio approached me with evident timidity; but a fiend-like glance from the G. K. imparted determination to the hearts of the death-dealing crew. The lantern was flaunted in close proximity to my face, as if to appal me with its skull and cross-bones. The gory ax was uplifted, but I was firm and quivered not.

The fellow with the rope now advanced, and by a most dextrous movement had me encoiled in his meshes of hemp, the uppermost coil materially interfering with my powers of respiration.

"Now we have the dastard!" shouted the G. K. "Brothers, witness the consummation of our noble Order's decrees."

Then

" There arose so loud a yell
  As if all the fiends from Heaven that fell
  Had raised the banner-cry of Hell!'

The G. K., with a look that seemed to penetrate my whole soul, said :

" Are you ready to pass through the ordeal presented ?"

Intimidated, as I must confess, by the scenes that surrounded me, I succumbed, and replied :

" Let your emissaries of real or feigned assault upon my person depart, and I am ready to proceed to the end."

In a moment the horrid trio disappeared, and the room was gleaming with light.

At once the Knights surrounded me, and the first to speak was my father :

" Son, thou hast acted nobly ; self-possessed and fearless, you have proven yourself worthy to be a true knight. Listen to and ponder well the tenth and final obligation about to be administered to you."

The G. K. now confronted me, and in a subdued but emphatic tone pronounced the following obligation :

" 10th. I, Edmund Wright, born of Southern parentage, and reared in the love and veneration of all the high-born institutions of the Southern States, and especially that of negro slavery, do now swear, in the presence of Almighty God, and of my brother Knights here assembled, that henceforth I will devote all the energies of my soul and body, without mental, physical or moral reservation, to the cause of the South ; against all aggressions upon her institutions by Abolitionists of the North ; and that I will regard all residents of the Northern States as Abolitionists at heart, and therefore inimical to the best interests of the South. And furthermore, I swear that the contemplated severance of the existing Union of the States is an imperative duty which I owe to my God, to the South, and to the natural supremacy of mind and social position over the mud-sills of humanity, be they black or white ; binding myself to this oath under the severest penalties it is possible for the mind of man to conceive, or human strength and skill to execute. So mote it be. In the name of God. Amen !"

" So mote it be. In the name of God. Amen !" is responded by all the Knights, three times repeated.

The G. K. then smote me with a sharp blow from his sword, and exclaimed:

" Arise, worthy Knight of the *Columbian Star*, and salute your peers and brothers."

One of the guides instructed me in the performance of this ceremony. He conducted me to a far corner of the inner room of the Temple, opened a small door, and introduced me to a splendid dressing-room. I was here clothed in helmet, a complete suit of armor, and presented with a handsome sword. The guide then reconducted me to the room we had just left, which had undergone so decided a change in my absence that I imagined for the moment we had entered a different apartment. The matter, however, was soon explained to my senses. The walls of the inner Temple were ingeniously draped with a heavy material, and painted in imitation of large columns and elegant frescoes. By a common mechanical contrivance, the drapery had been rolled up, disclosing a great number of niches in the real walls; and there, on my return, standing erect, still and silent, was a Knight in each niche, with helmet and armor like my own. The light was tempered to give this scene a very dramatic effect; and, as I was led three times around the Temple, giving me full opportunity to appreciate the best effect of such an exhibition, it occurred to me that I had never witnessed anything more solemnly grand and imposing. The armor was beautiful, and the helmets, each one of them surmounted by a golden crescent, in the center of which sparkled a brilliant jewel, looked like the crowns of true knights, who *deserved* to be engaged in a good cause.

This exhibition over, I was conducted to the center of the room and placed on a small platform. The G. K. then spoke as follows:

" Brave Knights! another star is added to our glorious constellation, and asks for a niche in the Temple of our heroes. Shall he ask in vain the reward of brave deeds at the hands of brave men?"

In unison of voice came the reply, slow and stern, from all the Knights:

"We carved these places for ourselves. Let yonder Knight do likewise."

" And so shall he," quickly responded the G. K. "Your hand, my brother. Come with me, and I will show you how brave deeds are rewarded here."

Hand in hand with the Grand Knight, I resumed my march around the Temple. As we were making our second circuit, we heard a voice that sounded as from one buried in the masonry of the walls:

"Ha! ha! a new Knight, but a coward! I'll fight him with a wooden dagger."

We stopped, and as I turned to look for some explanation of this strange challenge, a large sliding panel was moved aside, disclosing a beautiful throne, arranged in a niche, with a thousand fantastic decorations, and different in size and all its appointments from those occupied by the other Knights. Before the throne stood a strangely-appareled being, with helmet representing the head of an ass, and a huge wooden dagger in his hand.

"Ho, there he is! I smell his milky blood and chicken heart!" howled the beastly creature. "Most worthy Knight, why bring that child to me?"

"He is no child, Sir Ass, as thou wilt find. He wants the throne, and with the sword of his knighthood will make good his claim to it, or die the death."

"He shall die the death!" shouted Sir Ass.

"Go to your fate," said the G. K., addressing me, "and may God defend the right."

"May God defend the right," responded all the Knights.

I allowed myself to be pushed within the enclosure occupied by Sir Ass, and he stepped down to my level, bearing his wooden sword. Although I felt weak in the knees and imagined that my huge antagonist would soon crush me, the events I had just witnessed were sufficient to teach me that backing down would not help the case. I therefore determined to meet the issue with all the grace at my command.

The fight had every appearance of an earnest conflict, with life and death in the scale. Sir Ass was master of the weapon, and wielded it with a show of address that elicited my warmest admiration. After making a few passes that, to my poor judgment, were a wonder of skill and adroitness, he struck my sword a back-handed lick that sent it flying to the very ceiling, and left my arm wrenched and disabled.

"Down, coward!" he cried. "Beg for mercy before I drink your blood! Ha! ha! The craven squeal of the poor baby will be rare music!"

"Hold!" commanded the G. K. "Brothers! a Knight is in danger. To the rescue, Knights of the Star!"

"To the rescue, Knights of the Star!" was the general shout.

And they came with speed. Sir Ass was disarmed in a twinkling; and, before I had time to see how it was done, his strangely-helmeted head was rolling at my feet, dripping with gore! It looked like murder; and, well as I now know how the effect was produced, I can not, at this moment, recur to that barbarous scene without a great shudder of horror.

In the confusion the body was hurried from sight, so that, when I looked for the bleeding trunk, it was not there. The discovery was immediately made, however, that Sir Ass' successor must be elected at once, and I was not much surprised at my personal popularity when it was announced that I had been unanimously elevated to that position. I was conducted to the beautiful throne and placed upon it, with all the ceremonies and congratulations that men are accustomed to bestow upon the most famous. And then came a lecture on my duties; commands to be firm in the cause; threats of vengeance if I wavered; promises of great trusts and substantial advancements if I remained true—altogether making a *pot pourri* of blessings and damnings, whose principal ingredient seemed to be brimstone.

I have known for a long time that it *was* brimstone.

Then came the closing ceremonies, which, as they were very commonplace and silly, I have no occasion to record.

The only point that struck me as strange was the G. K. asking God to bless the Order and sanctify the hearts of its members. If such a thing as unpardonable blasphemy ever existed, it was then and there.

CHAPTER V.

SCHEMES of Knights holding high Official Positions in the Federal Capital—How
Stephen A. Douglas was Slaughtered by them—Red Rose Breckinridge
flaunts the Emblems of Treason under the nose of an Imbecile President
—Floyd, Toombs and Wigfall—Beauregard's intended Castle at West
Point—Dirty George N. Saunders—J D. B. and C. L. V.—A Cairo Rebel
Youth and a Peddling Spy—Terrible Atrocities on Tombigbee River—
Union Men and Women Smothered in a Cave—Blair, an inhuman Fiend,
renders his account to the Prince of Darkness—'Liza and Little Jack—The
Brains of a Child distributed.

Thus far I have endeavored to " show up," briefly, the existence
and inside workings of a mighty political organization, that is at
this moment secretly but industriously delving to undermine the
Government of our fathers. It is backed by wealth and power. Its
members stand in the halls of Congress, occupy positions of honor
and profit under the very Government they are plotting to subvert;
paralyzing our efforts to uphold the dear old flag, by employing
every means at their command to convey information of our plans
and movements to our armed foe.

They are scattered throughout the length and breadth of our
land—in every State, in every large city, and in many of the larger
towns—discouraging enlistments, counseling opposition to the
draft, advising repudiation of taxes, and poisoning public sentiment with all the murderous intent of an assassin!

They are the originators of conspiracies; the disciples of *habeas
corpus;* the " Not-another-man-nor-dollar " party of the North.

They are the foe in our midst, by whose insidious arts the minds
of thousands have been embittered against the model Government
of the world; by whose machinations the pure, fresh patriotism of
our youth has given way to an indescribable longing for some imaginary substitute of Republicanism, that will remain with them " the

evidence of things hoped for," till they find that "hope deferred maketh the heart sick."

You will find them daily on the streets and in all public places, holding their victims by the button-hole and filling their ears with tales of strange invention, corrupting love of country, and transforming it to sectional hate.

They are in our midst, like wolves in sheep's clothing, waiting only for the darkness they foretel and pray for, that they may drink our blood!

They are drinking our blood now!

Our blood, that flows in the veins of our sons and brothers, who now stand before the enemies of our flag!

They feast on the life-current that flows from the patriot's wounds, and rejoice at the wails of his dying agony. This in America to-day, under the ægis of freedom!

There can be no denial of these unpalatable facts, for have we not their effects fully upon us now; and have they not influenced the entire conduct of the present war? They *made* the war. Who will deny that the Knights of the Circle broke up the Charleston Convention; and that the breaking up of that assemblage was a foregone conclusion with them for weeks before its deliberations commenced? Who does not know that four years previously they defeated the popular candidate of that convention, Hon. S. A. DOUGLAS?

John C. Breckinridge was, and still is, one of the great lights of the K. G. C. He is indebted to the order for his nomination at Cincinnati on the Buchanan ticket, and for subsequent political advancement; and it is more by virtue of the "Red Rose" than any virtue of his own, that he now holds rank in the Confederate army. While Breckinridge was Vice-President of the United States, he publicly wore, in the City of Washington, the emblematic jewelry of this traitorous Order,—thus shamelessly parading his treason to the Government of which he was one of the principal officers! The same of Floyd, and Toombs, and Wigfall, and all their genus. In fact, Wigfall boasted publicly of the extent and power of the Order, and indulged in statistical enumerations of such a character, at Willard's, that it became necessary to close his mouth by special convention of such members of the Senate as had the inside track of the legislative cabal, and were entrusted with the keeping of the Order at the Capitol.

BEAUREGARD attempted the organization of a Castle at West Point, and really made some progress; but discoveries were made in time to discourage the carrying out of his purposes, and his removal prevented the renewal of the attempt. It is stated that some inkling of the designs of the Order reached the Government through these West Point operations, and that P. T. B. saved his distance only by the most dishonorable compromises of fact! He is doubtless one of the most industrious and scientific liars in the Southern Confederacy, and must have had large experience. In making this statement, I write from personal knowledge of a single fact and a thousand falsehoods!

FLYOD was the great light of the Washington Sanhedrim; and, without doubt, "J. B." was his prophet. GEO. N. SAUNDERS was intrusted with important commissions in the scavengers' department; and evidently felt honored while doing the dirty work of a few political hacks whose motto was "rule or ruin." Saunders was never trusted,—never admitted to important degrees in the League of the Circle;—and never considered worthy of position with Southern gentlemen, except to come at their whistle, and go at a jump when they cried "seek him!" As a dog, he has filled his position faithfully, and greedily devoured the crusts and bones that have been thrown to him from the Secession table.

J. D. B. proved himself a *bright* conspirator very early in the history of Golden Circles, and has held the position of chief fugleman, at the North, since the war commenced. He has said but little, and his hand has not been seen in the game; but he has played boldly, with his all at stake. His death, politically, is certain as his physical dissolution when he stops breathing, unless the Southern Confederacy establishes its independence. This he knows; and, with all the shrewdness of an old gamester, he is managing his trumps. C. L. V. was jealous of the prominence given to Jessie, years ago; and, with a fool-hardiness that astonished the most hardened of the Copperheads, he took a position, and uttered sentiments, that at once placed him in direct antagonism to the Government, and neutralized all his influence for mischief,—because, forsooth, the people are honest, and will not be led into error, except by chicanery. If the latter deserved banishment, the former should have been hung higher than Haman, years ago!

I am reminded not to deal in personalities. For myself, I would like to point out, by name, hundreds of people at the North, who

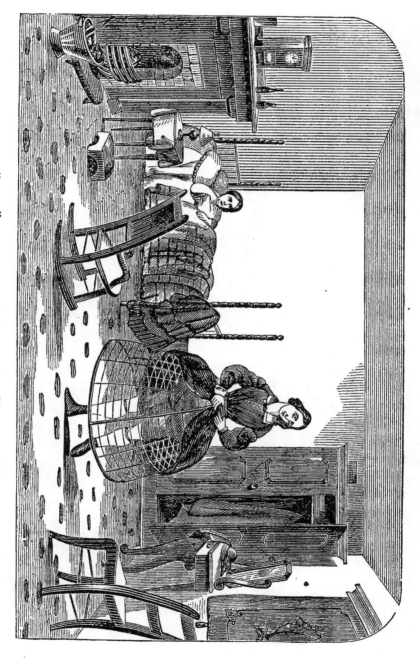

"SARY" PENETRATES MY DISGUISE—See page 112.

5

have done more toward prolonging this accursed war, in the interest of Secession, than thrice the same number at the South have accomplished ; but my publisher threatens to scratch all such items ; and incidents, without name or date, must therefore suffice.

I knew a man, in Indiana, sufficiently to recognize his countenance when I meet him (although I have never learned his name), that has been in the rebel capital, at least five times, since the beginning of the rebellion. He is a noisy Copperhead, and a leader among the Knights of the Circle, in his town. He has always rejoiced when the arms of the Union met with disaster ; and constantly predicts the dismemberment of our country. He admires Jeff Davis, and exalts him above every other man, which is going further than any Southerner I ever met. In fact, a majority of the people of the South express disappointment in Davis, and would gladly see another in his place ; but this Indiana rebel "out-Herods Herod," and would scout such an idea. Since the elections in Indiana and Ohio, I learn he is more quiet, and that he has abandoned the project of an immediate repetition of his visit to Richmond ;— I suppose from the fact that he promised the Northwest to the rebels, when last there ; and they will not readily discover that he has fulfilled the contract !

There is a youth at Cairo, whose recent history should furnish a short chapter in this record ; but, to make it complete, he should be more prominently individualized than my restrictions will allow. Perhaps enough of my readers will recognize a rough sketch to enable them to extract the fangs of the viper. He is a tall youth, with uncommonly broad shoulders, full face and blossoming proboscis. A very *open* countenance is partially hidden by red mustache and goatee ; while a huge guard chain and seals astonish every beholder with the immense respectability of the wearer. The youth has a wife (?) at St. Louis, mostly, although it is said he occasionally has one or two elsewhere !

When Cairo was threatened by the rebels, some two years ago, this valiant youth made a plan of the Union defenses there ; and showed therein, to a demonstration, what any fool could not help seeing, with the facts at his disposal, that a very small force could approach the town from the North, and possess it, in spite of any opposition the troops there could make. This plan was placed in care of a rebel spy, who had been amusing himself during the day by peddling cakes and apples among the troops, with no idea that

he was known and spotted almost from his first entrance into the
Union camp. As he was hurrying away, his course was interrupted,
and Mr. Spy, with the diagram of the Cairo fortifications in his
shirt pocket, slept in the guard-house that night, where he managed
to slip the document through a crack in the floor, undiscovered;
and from which he was honorably discharged, next morning, because the evidence was thought insufficient to warrant holding him.
The document was afterward found; and then a sleepy soldier,
who was on guard during the imprisonment of the suspected reb,
" allowed *that* was what he seed the peddler poking through the
crack; but he was mighty sleepy and didn't notice much."

It is not to my purpose to moralize on the awkwardness of the
proceedings in this case. The writing of the contraband document
was immediately recognized as that of the tall, broad-sholdered
youth, although it bore no name. It was decided to arrest him on
this evidence, and he *was* arrested; but, when the matter came up
for investigation, the naughty paper was *non est*, and several *interested* individuals were gratified with the discovery that there was
more than one Copperhead at Cairo, and that the uniform of U. S.
was not positive proof of a man's loyalty!

Since this event, the youth has been more careful; but he has
continued to work industriously for the success of the rebel cause;
and Jeff Davis has no more faithful slave than this Egyptian dough-
face. There are eyes upon his movements now, however, that will
detect rebellious lapses, and eventually hand him over to the fate
that will soon make the cultivation of hemp a more profitable em-
ployment.

This youth is the G. K. of the Cairo Knights.

There is a case of a woman in Cincinnati who has smuggled
thousands of dollars' worth of quinine, and other articles, for the
use of our enemies, since the war began. She was detected once,
and dismissed with a reprimand! What cares she for anything the
" mudsills" may say? Her husband is a Knight, and, when the
Confederacy triumphs, he will have a position, and madame will be
a lady.

But why make particular enumerations? Facts are patent to
the most ordinary comprehension that the worst rebels, and most
insidious enemies of our country, are at the North. Of course,
it is not here we witness the scenes of persecution and blood that
have earned for the Southern Knight the name of bandit and mur-

derer. It is not here we meet those red-mouthed ranters, who advocate the doctrines of Secession, without sugar-coating, or other new-light nostrum, to deceive the people. But in the North, we find the foe in ambush, or entrenched behind a secret order, whose deliberations are masked from the public gaze, and whose acts are the triumph of devils and the glory of hell!

Can any one who is informed, doubt the devilish origin of the Knights of the Circle? Had you been with me, to witness what I saw on the Tombigbee River, in the year of grace, 1861, when entire families were driven from their homes, as. though they were beasts of prey, or outlawed felons; driven to the woods and caves and swamps; old men, and weak women with infants at the breast, driven into the waters of the swollen river, to escape death by the trampling of horses' hoofs, as they came rapidly charging on the defenseless refugees; driven to a death little less horrible,—for I saw, at one time, seventeen men, women and children, drowned in that river, while fleeing from those they had for years been accustomed to look upon as their friends and neighbors; and, of the five who reached the opposite bank, two were shot dead by their pursuers, as they emerged from the waters tired and worn by their efforts to swim the rapid stream:

—Had you been forced, as I was, to assist in the stripping, torturing, and "final disposition" of an aged and respectable citizen of my native county,—a man that had been looked up to for half a century as one as the wisest and best; who had filled, to to the satisfaction of all who knew him, offices of honor and trust in our community; and who was now found to be obnoxious to the new-lights, because he could not indorse their their opinions:

If you could have seen the cruel and bloody murder of six brave men and women, in a small cave, in Southern Georgia,—attended by all the cruelties a savage would wreak on his most hated foe;—the shooting to death of innocent men and lovely women, in perfect wantonness:

Could you have witnessed so much of the workings of the Serpent in the Circle, you would not hesitate to agree with me that such an institution can not deny its devilish paternity, or that it is daily fulfilling the mission of its great progenitor.

But these little circumstances are only ordinary incidents in the history of the Knights,—of such frequent occurrence, except the last named, that they are no longer sufficiently exciting to please the tastes of the Crusaders; and their teeming brains are constantly at work to devise new plans of torture for the adherents of the Union. The murder of these people in the Georgia case, was a diversification of the general mode adopted by the chivalry to regulate the consciences of loyalists, and is deserving of particular mention.

At the point of the tale where the reader's interest is excited, full fifty horsemen were pursuing the party of six, also mounted, down the beautiful alluvion of an immense bayou. The chase had been long; the horses were miserably jaded and blown; and the riders of both parties seemed ready to drop from their saddles from exhaustion. It was a fearful sight: three men and three women, fleeing for life, before fifty reckless and bloodthirsty scoundrels, armed to the teeth, and exulting in an opportunity to commit murder in the name of law,—to shed blood with impunity, in the name of that foul abortion, the Southern Confederacy! The refugees espied a small cave across the bayou, overhung by projecting rocks; and at once made choice of it as the ark of their safety. It is their only hope; and, under a murderous fire from the pursuing force, they cross the shallow stream. One of the females of this doomed party was terribly wounded by a pistol shot that struck her as she reached the opposite bank; and to my dying day I shall not forget the expression of hopeless agony on her fair countenance, as she turned toward us. She dropped the reins, threw up her arms wildly, and seemed about to fall; then, with a sudden effort, she grasped the mane of her gallant steed, and urged him into the cave. The persecuted six, with their horses, were out of sight in a twinkling; and I felt like thanking God for their escape. They had not escaped, however; for unhesitatingly the mob plunged into the stream, and urged their beasts to the opposite shore.

"By hell, Blair, they are too deep for us," said a swarthy fellow, in white. "They are out of reach, now."

"Out of reach? No! I tell you, no! Damnation, man! do you suppose Pete Blair will be fooled now, till Andrews, and all the Andrews crew, have been sent to the devil? No!" he roared, in a voice of thunder, "not while there's powder and lead and cold steel, and courage enough to use them, left in Georgy. Out 'o them saddles, and what I tell ye to do, do that, and nothing else."

"But, Blair, let's save the wimmin," said white coat. "I don't feel right to run down defenseless females, and take their lives; and we havn't any right to kill 'em. Shoot both the Andrews Abolitionists—"

"By God, man! do you preach to me? Off that horse without another word, or I'll scatter your crazy brains where you'll find it inconvenient to scrape 'em up again. Down, all of you, and give me your pistols. There, now; all of you to work, and gather brush and dry wood to pile at the mouth of this hole. I'll smoke the groundhogs out, or roast them alive!"

The commands of the villain were rapidly obeyed, for all knew his desperate character; and, in all that crowd, there was not a man that did not fear him. While the men were thus busied, Blair amused himself by firing the pistols into the mouth of the cave; occasionally indulging in a boisterous laugh, as he discovered his shots were taking effect on the poor victims. He fired low, with the intention of maiming, so the agony of the poor wretches would be prolonged. In response to nearly every shot, came a piercing scream, followed by a groan of agony. It was rare sport for the slave trader, and he gloated over it, like an epicure over a choice morsel, indulging in oaths and gratulations too disgusting to repeat.

A huge stack of faggots was soon piled at the entrance of the cave, and there was lighted the funeral pyre of six as brave souls as ever suffered martyrdom for opinion's sake. There were murdered six gallant lives, because they loved the institutions of their fathers, and were loyal to the Government founded by Washington. But the work of vengeance commenced then and there, for one of the unfortunate victims succeeded in crawling forward to a position where he took certain aim, and sent a bullet crashing through the brain of the monster, Blair! The big rebel fell heavily, and was dead on the instant, for I stood near, and turned him over at once to discover the extent of the wound. He breathed, perhaps, slightly; but by no other sign intimated that the moment before he was full of life and brute force, and the terror of fifty desperadoes. Life flickered for a second or two in the uncouth socket, and then a human soul went out into the darkness of death, to encounter the dread uncertainties of a hopeless eternity!

The men gathered around the dead monster, and gazed upon him shyly, evidently treasuring the recollection of his great power and determination while in life, and astonished that even death should master him. It was a strange picture,—rough and uncouth, without doubt, in many appointments, and horrible in detail; but who shall say it was not the appropriate finale of a bad life, hurried to its doom without an opportunity to repeat the acts of which it even now carried the damning evidence of guilt to the great judgment? The men came nearer; and when they found that Pete Blair was really dead, they gazed into each other's faces with stupid wonder, muttered unmeaning comments on his fate, and roughly criticized the demoniac expression of his grim visage.

"Pete and old Andrews will have a close race on the road to hell!" said white coat. "But Pete is entitled to odds, for he is on foot, and Andrews has a beast."

I was astonished at such a speech on such an occasion, but more than half of those present set up a boisterous laugh at what they seemed to consider a good joke; and the hilarity of the occasion was greatly increased by similar remarks from several of the party.

"The devil will certainly resign when Pete gets there," said John Morrow; "or, mabbe he'll take him in pardner, and increase the business. With such a devil as Pete would make, we'd have a hell worth talking about!"

"Mr. Devil must look sharp for his niggers," said another; "for Pete will cheat him out of the lot in a jiffy, if he allows any trade at all. He sold me a nig onct for tu thousand, and then told my neighbor, Joe Pierson, that that nig had the smallpox. Joe tried to raise hell, and have the nig killed or tuk away; but Pete come around jest in time to buy him back, for five hundred. He couldn't pay no more, kaise he couldn't afford to lose no more on one nig; but the same week he made the same kind of a trade with that very nigger, along with Miran Curtis,—gittin' tu thousan' agin, and then buying back for five hundred. The truth is, thet nig was posted in the smallpox business, and was wuth a fortune to any sharp trader, like Pete. He made a world of money with him."

The crowd laughed and cheered. In their estimation, no more fitting eulogy could be passed on the dead!

"Well, boys, 'spose we put him under," suggested White Coat. "We may as well plant him here, right now; and then we'll poker for his hoss and nigs, unless we can agree on a division. I'll take

RUINS OF MY HOME—See page 147.

the gal, 'Liza Jane, if you're all agreed, and you may fight out the balance."

" No yer don't, by God!" shouted Bill Streeter, who was a small trader in contrabands. " Yer don't take thet gal wile I'm alive; *shore;* an' don't yer try it on."

"Pshaw, Bill," responded white coat; "I didn't 'spose you'd have Pete's cast off trash, at any price. In course, if *you* want the gal, I've nothen' to say, only thet you'll get her and keep her, in spite of everybody." ·

"That I will, *shore.* Dus any man say contrary?"

No!

It was immediately manifest that Bill Streeter was now the bully of the mob, *ex-officio.* The " coming man " had arrived to assume the leadership of these peoples, and the care of 'Liza Jane. There he was, a great miserable, whisky bloat, with pistols in his belt, a huge butcher-knife sticking in his boot, and an immense whip buttoned to his sides, as the badge of his profession! He was there, *shore.*

Bill Streeter, I am sorry to record, is not the type of a small class at the South. He is a representative man in Southern society, whose peers and confreres give shape and tone to public sentiment, and manage the politics of Governments; who direct and control the Secession elements that are now warring against freedom; who

> "Treason and murder ever kept together,
> As two yoke-devils, sworn to cither's purpose;
> Working so grossly in a natural cause,
> That admiration did not whoop at them ; "

Who are the devil's servants, and, as Knights of the Golden Circle, wear his chosen livery !

"Dig a hole in the sand there, to plant Pete Blair in," said White Coat; "and then we'll proceed to business; eh, Bill?"

"Throw old Blair on the fire and let his damned carcase roast!" said Streeter. "We can't fool away time with a dead scoundrel, like him."

And before a few of the better disposed in the mob could interfere, Blair's pockets were rifled, everything of value stripped from his person, and his bloody remains pitched into the fire with as little ceremony as though he had been a worthless log!

This was the funeral of a Knight of the League, as conducted by his brother Knights and compatriots in the cause of the South. Can the institutions that sanction such proceedings ever prosper?

Then, in sight of his smouldering flesh and bones, these inhuman devils sit in a circle to divide the dead man's effects. Pete had no relatives; and therefore these, *his best friends*, were the natural inheritors of his estate. Streeter took direction of matters, and, without so much as asking leave, chose for himself the quadroon girl, 'Liza Jane, and the pet horse, Devileye. Nobody thought of raising an objection. He then asked the crowd to nominate two persons to play a game of poker for the second choice; and, after much noisy profanity and foul recrimination, White Coat and Charley Lowndes took their seats in the ring, produced a greasy "Mississippi Bible," and went in for a share of the spoils. White Coat a-head, and he chose a mulatto girl that he told me, in confidence, was as good as the quadroon, only not quite as well-looking.

Then John Morrow played with Charley, and won the black stallion; and so on, 'till every member of the gang had possessed himself of some relict of the departed bravo. I wished to decline participating in this horrid ceremony, but Streeter swore every man should go in regularly for his share, or fight; and, knowing the odds were very largely against me, I went in, of course. I chose a young house-servant that I knew very well, merely as a matter of form, never, for a moment, expecting to take him; but, when we returned to Pete's ranche, Streeter led him out and handed him over with a style that told me, plainly as it could have been expressed in words, that I would refuse him at my peril.

The ceremony of announcing Blair's death, and the immediate parceling out of his estate, on our return, was a singular admixture of the tragic and comic, that made an indelible impression on me. When the quadroon was informed of her master's fate, she replied:

"Golly! don't tell? Mars' Pete dun gone dead! Ump! if nig told dat, wud be dam lie!"

"Haw!" laughed Streeter; "thet's good. 'Liza Jane don't b'lieve Pete's gone tu hell. It's a *shore* thing, gal; an', what's more, you're my nigger."

"Your nig, Mars' Streakery? oh, no; no, no! doan't say dat, good Mars'; doan't say dat!"

"Don't? Why not, you Satan's imp? I say you're my nig,

shore; an' ef yer breathe a word agin it, I'll string ye up, by God!"

"No, Mars' Streakery, I'se not gwine ter say no more gin' it; but, good Mars', let me ax yer, *whose nig's little Jack?*"

"Who got·'Liza's Jack, boys? Did anybody take him? No? Wal, somebody must, fer I'm damned ef I keep the brat. - Divide once more, an' see who gets him."

'Liza was Jack's mother, and the dead Blair was his father! He was seven years old, and a very smart little curley-headed, brown-cheeked rogue—carrying the impress of his mother's beauty and his father's health, in his handsome face. He was the very apple of his mother's eye, and she had made it her special mission, since his birth, to see that he was well-cared for, and shielded from all harm. When Streeter made the heartless announcement that he would part the mother and child, 'Liza darted across the yard, where little Jack was enjoying himself at play with other children, and grasping him in her arms, ran, with the fleetness of a deer, toward the woods. She had made a bad reckoning, however, if she stopped to reason at all; for Streeter at once bounded into his saddle, and pursued her at full speed. In such a race there could be but one result. 'Liza was soon overtaken, felled to the earth by a blow from the huge fist of the maddened villain, who kicked and pounded her, in a very frenzy of rage, till she was insensible. He then seized little Jack by his long hair, remounted his horse, and rode back to us at the same breakneck pace. The screams of the boy were truly heartrending, and but few in that crowd that did not express their horror of such a proceeding; but the climax of dreadful crimes was yet reserved to freeze the blood of every man present, who had a spark of humanity left in his heart. Streeter rode up to the assemblage, cast the boy with great force to the ground, dismounted, and seizing him by the feet, swung him in the air two or three times around very swiftly, and then, with all his strength, brought the tender infant head crashing against the horse-block! The little fellow's brains and blood were scattered in the faces and on the clothing of those who stood near; and the scene presented at that moment was one of the most startling horror ever witnessed out of the infernal regions. Pitching the lifeless corpse into our midst, the monster yelled:

"There he is. Yer kin divide him now without trouble, *shore,* an' git ekil shares!"

"Bill Streeter!" shouted Charley Lowndes, "you've done a thing now that the devil himself will be ashamed of. That's murder, or I'm a liar!"

"Hush, Charley," said an old man, standing near me. "We have had blood enough for one day, and we can't spare you yet."

Several of the more peaceably disposed now interfered, and induced Streeter to go into the house. He was led along like a mad bull, under keepers, or a jackal that had just scented blood, and was crazy to feast on it.

"Something must be done with the boy," suggested Charley. "'Liza will get back in a little while, and it won't do to have Jack lying here then. We must plant him out of sight."

One of the men wrapped the murdered boy in a coarse blanket, and bore him away beyond the cabins. About a dozen followed, myself among the number; and in a beautiful ravine, shaded by cypress and palmetto, we buried the mangled body of the innocent child, just as the sun was shedding his last faint rays over the homes of men. That little grave is in the State of Georgia, a monument of more significance to-day than any marble shaft within her borders! I saw 'Liza no more; but can faintly imagine the scene when she returned, and found the light of her life extinguished, and herself the forced paramour of her child's murderer! My God! can such things be, in this age of enlightened liberty?

As we came up from the burial of Jack, we encountered a scene of a far different character from any I had yet witnessed. Quite an assemblage was gathered around White Coat and a bright mulatto woman, and the sport was rare, judging from the shouts of laughter that greeted us as we drew near.

"Certainly, Jule; yer my nigger. Yer the first choice of the lot, and I was bound to have yer at any cost," said White Coat.

"Wat yer want uv me, hoss? Yer ain't got no fam'ly, an' I doan't like ter lib wid a bach'lor, kase people might *talk*, yer know."

"But we'll soon hev a family, Jule, and then you'll hev plenty of company, for thar's a heap of people on my place. You'll—"

"*We'll* hev fam'ly, did yer say? Who'm *we*? You, mars', an' me, Jule? Whoop! Haw! haw! haw! dat beat de debbil!" and, with a sudden spring, she clasped White Coat about the neck with her great arms, and throwing her legs about him, above the hips, she forced him to one of the spiciest embraces a white man ever received. At the same time she slobbered great Ethiopian kisses on his face and lips, interspersing the ceremonies with wild yells of delight, and sharp kicks in the neighborhood of his strongest emotions. \Her poor victim was in a perfect ecstasy of rage. He swore and threatened and begged by turns; still the somber kisses and the wild caress.

Of course, the spectators of this performance enjoyed it deliciously. They yelled and screamed and squealed, and threw themselves into grotesque positions; and, withal, it was a scene that beggars description, and would require sufficient canvas for a panorama to reproduce.

"Wal, mars', yer's nigh gin eout," said Jule, at length, "an' reckon yer had 'nuff dis. Dar's no use in world bein' mad an' bitin' yerseff, for wat's dun is dun gone, *shore*. Yer won't hurt dis nig, mars', will yer, ef I let's yer go?"

"Hurt yer! damned if I don't cut yer black throat!" screamed White Coat.

"No, no, he shan't hurt yer," said a chorus of voices. "Kiss him jest a leetle more, Jule, and then let up. We'll take car' of *him!*"

Jule kissed very slyly, then braced herself and gave a powerful spring backward. She struck on her feet in good order, but White Coat went summersaulting backward like a sugar-hogshead, making many hopeless efforts to preserve his equilibrium, and finally brought up posteriorwise, with his head butting a turpentine barrel. The crowd gathered about him as he straightened himself to his perpendicular, and the great cheer with which they rent the air was lustily given.

The poor victim was mad enough, but he had the good sense to restrain himself, and finally joined in the laugh.

"Any man that wants that nig., for five hundred, kin jest take her, and be damned," said he.

"Then, she's mine," shouted Charley Lowndes; "and, gentlemen, remember she's under my protection. You will all agree that she was put up to do this little thing that's jest over, and she's not to be harmed for it."

"All right, Charley; we'll see fair play;" and Lowndes was at once the popular man of the crowd.

It may be wondered why I, who make some professions of decency, was a witness of the horrors I have herein very imperfectly described. I was induced to join this God-defying mob, only by the argument the wily and unscrupulous slave-driver always uses: Force! Blair had been a negro-trader for many years; had imported several cargoes by his own personal exertions, and was rich from the spoils of blood. His associates were of his own stamp; blood-thirsty pirates, and heartless scoundrels; secessionists from interest, and Knights of the Golden Circle in due sequence.

This delectable crowd raised a hue and cry against the fealty of James Andrews, Senior and Junior, and Robert Thompson, old citizens of Georgia, to the sacred cause of the South. This, however, was all sham, and the real cause of enmity a matter of a quite different description. Blair had defrauded Andrews by selling him three negroes, that he warranted several years younger than they were; and a vexatious law-suit was the result. The day for final trial drew nigh; and Blair, discovering the weakness of his defense, and probable discomfiture, swore that Andrews should die before the session of the court.

He devised many plans to destroy the life of his victim; and spread the report industriously, that he was an abolitionist of the most objectionable stripe. Such a report, once believed, was equivalent to a sentence of death; and, among the mob controlled by Blair, it gained easy credence, of course.

On the day in which the scenes I have just described were enacted, a spy, employed by Blair, had made the discovery that the two Andrews and Robert Thompson, with their wives, were riding to a distant friend's, to spend the day. The mob was immediately mounted and started in pursuit, pressing into their service all stragglers and chance equestrians they found in their course. I, being among the stragglers, was forced to accompany these scoundrels, and unwillingly assist in one of the most heartless murders that stains the annals of crime.

My description does not do it justice, but enough is described to show the diabolical purposes of those miscreants, who assume the name of Knights to cover their damnable transgressions of justice and right.

MURDERING UNIONISTS IN RANDOLPH COUNTY, GEORGIA.

CHAPTER VI.

CREDULITY of a noble veteran Southerner—Perception of a Yankee Wife—She outgenerals in argument her newly-knighted Spouse—The Turning Point—St. Augustine Castle—Commission for the Establishment of new Temples—Villainous Designs, most widely known, the sooner exposed.

"ONCE a Knight, always a Knight," is a standing axiom of the Order. When you go in, you know not what you are doing, but are led along step by step, to assume obligations, word by word and sentence by sentence, that every honest man would scout with scorn, could he see them as a whole and scan their tendencies deliberately.

A few days after I had taken the obligation of the Columbian Star degree, I sat down to think the matter over, and the more I thought the less I liked it.

There was no point from which I could view the machinery of this institution, and obtain a favorable impression of its objects. All looked dark, bloody and seditious; and I felt that I had engaged in a cause that would never find favor in the sight of God.

My father, poor old man, had evidently been actuated by the best of motives in connecting himself with the order, for he looked upon it, as did thousands of others, as the only salvation of the South. It had come to be a very popular belief that the South needed an extraordinary amount of salvation, and her chivalric sons were not slow to pledge themselves in her behalf.

I would gladly have conferred with some one, my father in preference to all others, regarding my doubts of the efficacy of the Knights for good; but the obligations I had assumed, and by which I then felt bound, debarred me this privilege. I was sorely troubled, without prospect of relief, when it occurred to me that, under cer-

tain restrictions, I might talk on the subject with my wife. I therefore introduced the subject in the most embarrassing form, by
saying:

"Lucy, I wish to tell you a secret."

"Really, husband, you almost frighten me. A *real* secret? I
had no idea you would keep anything from me—a secret, especially."

"Confidentially—for your ear alone; mind now, not a word to
another living soul. I have joined the—"

"Knights of the Golden Circle," she interrupted. "My! what
a secret! I've known that ever since it happened, and have wanted
to ask you, several times, what they do at their meetings, and what
they did with you, dear man, when you first went. Tell me all
about it now."

"I can not tell you that; it is a secret."

"But you wanted to tell me a secret, and haven't done it. Proceed, if you please."

"I am not allowed to tell, even if I wished. And then it is not
an Order in which ladies are supposed to be interested."

"Probably not; but you are not doing acts you are ashamed of,
I hope?"

"I can not even answer such a question as that."

"Indeed? What a horrible society! But, Edward, you do not
give me credit for sufficient perception. I can see that you are
troubled, and that your trouble commenced when you connected
yourself with these Knights. You will not deny that there is
something wrong about them, and that you prefer to be released
from the obligation of your compact. Recollect that an obligation
taken under constraint is not binding on your honor nor your conscience; and that, if you are convinced it is wrong, the sooner it
is retracted and repented of, the better for you and all that love
you."

"Your words assume more than I am prepared to admit; but I
will say to you, what I would not have another living soul hear
from my lips, for the world, that I do not like my connection with
this league, and would retract, could I do so with safety and honor."

"The time will surely come, then, when you will find the con-
servation of safety and honor in no other course. I have regretted
your union with this order from the beginning, because I saw its
principles were not in accordance with yours, and that the incon-

gruity occasioned you much annoyance. Your countenance and acts told me all this, as plainly as words could have told; and, if you do not want all the world to know what troubles you, you must wear a better mask."

My wife had really outgeneraled me, and knew all my weak points. I had nothing to tell, for she already knew more than I would then impart.

Troubles, it is said, never come singly. My father's health had been very indifferent for years, and of late he seemed to decline rapidly.

One night, near the time of the above described conversation with my wife, my mother called me, in great alarm, saying he was much worse and needed immediate attention. After dispatching a trusty messenger for physicians, I took my place at his bedside, and did not leave him till he had breathed his last, late the succeeding day.

This event was the turning point in my career.

By my father's will, I learned his desire that I take as my homestead a fine plantation he owned in the neighborhood of St. Augustine, Florida; and, soon as I had arranged affairs to leave, I moved thither, and took up my abode.

Immediately on my arrival I was waited upon by several Knights of the Circle, to whom I had been reported from my Castle, and whose mission was to urge my immediate connection with them. When I requested a little time for consideration, and to become somewhat acquainted, I was abruptly told it would not be allowed; that I was not viewed at home as being any too sound, and that I was expected to prove my faith by my works without delay. So I made a virtue of necessity, by immediate application for admittance to the St. Augustine Castle, and was entered on the books thereof.

I had been here but a few weeks when I was appointed one of a special commission to institute and organize several new Castles in different parts of the South.

With a ready acquiescence, and apparent hearty determination to forthwith commence the organization of new Temples, I invited my fellow-commissioners to meet me for consultation as to the most eligible points at which it would be judicious to feel the sentiments and foregone conclusions of men, in all ranks of life, as to whether they had yet heard of the existence of the Order, and if so, what opinions had they formed as to its purposes and merits.

The commissioners met in due time at my newly-acquired mansion. I had casually remarked to my wife that I expected company that evening and wished not to be disturbed for an hour or two.

At once the truth flashed across her mind, and she said in an imploring tone:

"Edmund, I fondly hoped that upon the death of your father, a highminded, but misled gentleman, you would discontinue all connection with the unholy institution whose acts so imbittered the closing hours of his life."

Her remark somewhat startled me and I replied:

"It is true, that father was a knight of the order, but he never by word or act gave me the slightest intimation that he had cause to regret his connection with the institution, and why do you speak as you do?"

My wife sadly responded:

"Edmund, I will tell you why when we are next alone; but your expected company are at the door."

The party was composed of six knights, whom, after a passing introduction to my wife, I led to my private apartment. After the usual formalities of recognition as brother knights, we proceeded at once to the business of our commission, and by unanimous assent I acted as chairman. When and where shall our noble order locate new temples was of course, the main question. At once there was an evident diversity of opinion. It had so happened that not two members of the conclave claimed birthright in the same State, and each put in his claim for the undoubted loyalty of the State of his nativity to the institutions of the South and the contemplated confederacy.

After much discussion and contention it was decided that new temples should be established as follows: three in Texas, two in Arkansas, four in Tennessee, one in Kentucky, three in Maryland, and one in Delaware; each member to determine the cities or towns in which the new temples should be located. Thus it will be seen that six States were represented, and the apportionment was allotted upon what seemed to be an equitable basis, Tennessee being deemed as more especially in need of salvation. Now came my turn to select, and with deference to me as president it was voted that I was at liberty to locate six temples.

The reader will doubtless be somewhat astounded when I assert that I announced my determination to locate all my six Temples in Northern States, namely, one in each of the following : Ohio, Indiana, Illinois, New Jersey, Michigan and Maine. Now for my reasons for so doing.

Fully convinced of the hellish purposes and blasting influences of the Order, I had arrived at a fixed determination, step by step, as opportunities presented, to unvail the mysteries and enormities of the most devilish institution ever conceived of by creatures bearing the semblance of humanity.

Having arrived at the conclusion, after due deliberation with my sense of right, that villainy unmasked, and its purposes most widely known, would more readily be exposed to the gaze of the honest masses, and its influences for evil, the sooner counteracted, I imagined that a knowledge of the Order in the North might effect good rather than evil. True, I was aware that Temples had already been organized in several of the Northern States, but I well knew that they were controlled by men as inimical to the Union as the veriest venom-spitting Copperheads in South Carolina.

However, the acts of the commission had yet to be approved by St. Augustine Temple, and its action upon the recommendations of the commission will be stated in the due course of this narrative.

CHAPTER VII.

Advice of a Dying Knight—Removal of the Author to Georgia—Confidence in a Northern Woman—A Letter that told—The North has an inkling of Traitorous Schemes—Extinction of Slavery must bide its time—How Patriots Write—Summons to St. Augustine Castle.

Soon as my brother Knights had departed, after our convention, the proceedings of which are detailed in the last chapter, I hastened to my wife's apartment, eager to hear her explanation as to what might have been said to her by my father with reference to the Order.

She seemed, on the instant, to anticipate the object of my hasty entrance, and probably her countenance betokened a look that indicated a recollection of our late conversation.

"Edmund," she said, "I promised to tell you, when next we were alone, how I knew that your father's connection with the Golden Circle embittered the closing hours of his life. You are aware that during several days and nights I sat by his bedside, soothing, in my feeble way, the mortal sufferings he endured. A day or two before his death he intimated that he wished to impart to me some cause of remorse before he was removed from earth. Speaking in a suppressed voice, he said:

"'Daughter, though by birth of Northern parentage and sentiments, all of which I once detested, I am now convinced that you are well deserving of the affections of my son, and the only member of my family to whom I dare impart, with full confidence in your discretion and secrecy, a deliberately-formed conviction of my mind, and one deeply associated with the duty I owe to my country. By my will Edmund will learn that, after providing for his mother, the bulk of my fortune has been bequeathed to him and to yourself, with an expressed desire that your home will be, after my

"GWO UP ER DOWN, G—D D—N YER, QUICK."—See page 130.

departure, at my favorite estate in St. Augustine, Florida, as connected with it are many slaves over whom I wish to leave, not only a kind master and mistress, but such protectors as will advise and defend them in the convulsion which is but too apparent to my vision in the near future. Recently I have written the letter which I now hand you. Soon after you are domiciled in your new home, hand the letter to Edmund; but, as it is yet unsealed, you are at liberty to peruse its contents.' "

Knowing, of course, the full tenor of my father's will, but not imagining that he had left any other document for my especial interest or attention, I eagerly caught the letter presented, and in a moment devoured its contents.

Thus runs the letter, which I have sacredly kept, and of which no power on earth can rob me, so long as physical strength remains to enable me to retain possession of the last and most highly prized gift of my now departed and, I trust, sainted parent:

THE LETTER.

" *My Dear Son Edmund:*

" Convinced that the hour is nigh, when, by the will of an All-wise Creator, my earthly career must terminate, I feel it imperative upon me as a duty I owe to my God, to my country and to you, and from the performance of which my conscience admits of no evasion, to divulge to you the last and only matter not yet arranged with God and man.

" My feeble hand admonishes me to be brief; and, in a word, the cause of my disquietude is my connection with that institution known as the Knights of the Golden Circle, and into whose soul-destroying meshes I have been the instigation of your entanglement, contrary to the impulses of your noble nature.

" Until now I dared not say to you what, as a father, I *must* say. Had I done so when first impressed with a conviction of grievous error, well do I know that your better judgment would have accorded with mine, too long deferred; but the innate love of right which marks your character would have induced you to

" ' Right such wrong, where'er 'twere given,
' E'en 'twere in the Court of Heaven.'

" The consequence of the attempt would have been to you and to me, death—inglorious death.

" About to face the last enemy of man, I waive all fear and trust to your discretion to escape from the toils by which you are encompassed, without encountering the perils which will beset you in the effort.

" Let all earthly affairs be subservient to your speedy withdrawal, consistent with your personal safety, from that most unrighteous institution, under whose influences you have, by my means, been brought.

" It is a cabal conceived in Hell, nurtured by the arch-fiend, accursed of God, and soon to be by all honest men.

" These, my parting words, are intrusted to our dear Lucy, from whom I have learned more lessons of wisdom than were ever taught me by man or woman of Southern affinities.   To her gentle and truthful counsels I earnestly commend you.   YOUR FATHER."

Had there lingered in my bosom one only doubt as to what course I should pursue, the letter of my father removed it.

Denunciation, denouncement and exposure, seemed to comprise my whole vocabulary.

Domestic duties incident to my change of residence demanded my attention, and with them, and pleasant converse with my wife, time, in its never ceasing round, rolled pleasantly onward.

Letters from home reached my wife, and I could well imagine that at least some of them were in response to others from her. With the native intuition of the Yankee mind, there ran a vein through many of the epistles that she might not be quite happy in her Southern home.

An inkling of the existence of the Circle had evidently reached the " hub of the universe," and the knowledge of the fact must soon be broadcast throughout all that region in which reign supreme the noble attributes of reason, right, intelligence and freedom of mind untrammeled.

Especially was I forcibly stricken with questions in one of the letters.   They were as follows :

" Lucy, does Edmund still evince that high and noble bearing, that exuberance of affection, which so marked his character when here, and which compelled us all to love him as one of 'Nature's noblemen?'   While none of our family doubt it, there are those in the circle of our social relations, who at times furtively throw out hints that, perhaps, Edmund might not, after all, be the man he professed and appeared to be.

"Strange rumors are afloat, especially among our leading statesmen and politicians, that there is some convulsion in the nation, but the nature of which no man seems to have any lucid idea, is about to occur.

"We all feel that the question of negro slavery is one of great delicacy, and that the people of the South are too apt to consider all citizens of the North as radical Abolitionists. This, you know, is not the fact.

"Revolutionary memories compel us to love our brothers and sisters of the sunny clime; and, to the unerring laws of civilization, the wise legislations of our national councils, in which Southern statesmen have ever had so large a share, and, above all, to the all-wise dictates of an overruling Providence, we are ever willing to leave the final settlement of the momentous question."

In another letter, of later date, occurs this paragraph:

"Gossip is still rife as to real or imaginary troubles, ere long to arise between the two sections of the country, growing out of the slavery question. Some have gone so far as to intimate that a secret organization exists in the South, and that spies have for years been among us, prying into the acts of our people, both public and private, preparatory to some important movement. If such an organization exists, or any such unholy scheme has been conceived of, we all hope that your husband has too much patriotism to be drawn into a vortex which will surely redound to the ruin of at least one section of our now happy country, if not ruinous to the whole nation."

These letters convinced me forcibly that the North knew more than the South could possibly imagine.

Here was I in a strait, my loyalty as a Knight doubted in the South, and my devotion to the Union at least suspected in the North; but the time, I well knew, was at hand, when I would be summoned to a conclave of St. Augustine Castle, and its summons must be obeyed, for I was to report as chairman of the commission.

To leave the order was, of course, my fixed determination, but I must, as a matter of personal safety, bide my time.

Brooding over the state of affairs, my revery was broken by a faithful old slave of my father, who handed me a sealed note. The

device on the seal told me at once as to whence it emanated.   It
was the expected summons to attend a called meeting of St. Augustine Castle.

My report of the deliberations and conclusions of the commission as to the most advisable locations of new Temples, had to be
prepared, and my time was limited.

Hastily I wrote the report, doubtful whether it would meet with
the favor of the G. K., and those who would be actuated by his
opinions.

Little did I know that all the labors of myself and fellow-commissioners had been of no avail.   The report was never submitted,
for astounding intelligence had reached the Order from the Lone
Star State, as will be learned by the reader, in the next chapter.

CHAPTER VIII.

HERESY at Galveston—Detectives—Sealed Instructions—Ex-Clergyman Knight —A sound Judge—Galveston Knights too smart for St. Augustine—Fool's Errand—Postoffice not public—Experience therein—Acts of the Triumvirs—"Under the Pump"—"March of the Crescent"—Detectives in "durance vile."

AT a called meeting of San Augustine Castle, that had been hastily summoned for special business, reports were read and complaints duly entered that strange irregularities were practiced by Knights in different localities, but more especially at Galveston. The work of the order was materially changed by would-be reformers, and all its machinery remodeled to suit the new programme. Here was heresy; an occasion to test the inquisitorial power of our jesuitical cabal to the utmost, and firmly establish its efficiency for self-regulation. It was resolved to meet the issue boldly, by extreme measures, that would prove a severe lesson in the present, and a wholesome check to future tergiversations; but, to be able to meet it fairly, the extent of these mal-practices, by whom introduced and sustained, and all the grounds of the substitution, must be more clearly defined; otherwise, so it was argued, we might endanger the prestige of our own work, by running counter to an influence as powerful as our own. The Solons of our Castle were doubtless sufficiently discreet, and wisely cautious, as the result will prove.

It was gravely determined, after much deliberation, to establish a corps of detectives (a smoother name for spies), to act in concert with detectives of other regular Castles in ferreting out the source and extent of the irregularities complained of, and report thereon without delay. Immediate action seemed necessary, for the danger was increasing daily. It was, therefore, resolved to send from San Augustine to Galveston a force of three special detectives, who should also be commissioners with plenary powers to enforce the established regulations of the order, should it be found

necessary and expedient, after due investigation. Reports, however, were to be made daily, and instructions waited for on all
points not sufficienlty clear to the commission."

It was certainly opposed to my wishes, although flattering to my
pride, to receive the nomination as one of the spies ; for it was an
honor sought after by many Knights who were doomed to disappointment. My companions in the mission were men of mature
years and ripened judgment; an ex-judge and a superannuated
itinerant, retired on ample fortunes, and very respectable, dignified and corpulent. We were directed to retire for conference;
make arrangements for an early departure, and report to the Castle for final instructions. The Knights would await our return.

Preliminaries were settled without delay, and it was determined
to start on the following morning. Instructions were promised to
be in readinoss at that time, and we were excused from further at-
tendance on the meeting, that we might complete preparations for
departure.

Subsequent events will explain why I have jotted down these
particulars, many of which, at first glance, seem unimportant and
common-place.

Next‑morning we were early at the place of rendezvous, and
were met by the G. K., who delivered to each of us a sealed packet,
with instructions "not to open till we arrived at Galveston ; not to
confer regarding their contents, except in the event of a contingency
therein set forth ; and, on pain of suffering the penalty denounced
against recusant Knights, not to exhibit our instructions, one to the
other, nor to any living soul. Instructions were in cipher, the key
to which he would impart verbally, under the strongest injunc-
tions to secresy. If we were sufficiently wary, industrious and discreet, he felt assured our mission would not be entirely barren of
good results ; but we must always keep in view the best good of
the order, and make every personal sacrifice to preserve its great
principles firm and intact. It would be expected of us to keep
clear of avoidable dangers, provided duties could be performed as
efficiently by so doing; but our lives and all our possessions were
the property of the order whenever it choose to claim them, and if
it became necessary to risk all now, we must not hesitate. In
taking leave of us, the G. K. said: ·

"Brother Knights—I will not disguise from you that I view your
mission with great interest, for it is important, and on its success

TALBOT'S LAST INTERVIEW WITH MRS. WRIGHT.—See page 145.

7

depend, in some degree, the destinies of an Empire. We send you forth with full reliance in your judgment and patriotism; and have no doubt that whatever man can do, under the peculiar circumstances of your appointment, you will faithfully and industriously accomplish. I shall look impatiently for your first report, and shall hail your success with emotions of hearty gratitude."

We were off. The journey was pleasant, and full of agreeable incident; and the great business of our journey seemed to have been forgotten by all, or purposely ignored, in the more entertaining pastime of story-telling and card-playing. We were a true Southern party—jovial, boisterous and hearty—and bound to make the most of our opportunities to-day, whatever might be the effect on to-morrow. "Let to-morrow take care of itself, as long as there's whisky in the jug," was the motto of a fine old Southern gentleman, and it would make a good motto for the Southern Confederacy, if they had whisky enough left to be worth referring to.

Not till we saw the lights of Galveston, as we were sailing up the bay, did my companions allude to the object of our journey. The old Judge looked out and remarked:

"We're nearly there. I hope this is not a fool's errand, and was not disposed to view it as such when we started; but, gentlemen, it has occurred to me that there are men in Galveston *almost* as smart as some of our common people at Augustine; and, if we get a-head of them, it will be more good luck than superior wit that should have the credit. If we follow instructions, nothing more can be reasonably expected, and probably will not be looked for; but I have some ambition to meet the desires of our Castle to the last fraction, and have no doubt you join me in the feeling."

" Of course circumstances must guide us, more or less," said the Reverend, "without proceeding outside of instructions. But the instructions themselves will, doubtless, give us what light we need, and we must abide by them. I am fully confident we shall effect something for the good of the order, if we put our trust in Providence, and do our duty as pointed out."

"For myself," said I; "I have little ambition to gratify; but, as I have accepted the trusts of this appointment, my best efforts shall be devoted to the accomplishment of its purposes, so far as I can reconcile those purposes to my consciousness of right and my duty to God."

"Consciousness of right and duty to God!" exclaimed the ex-clergyman. "You do not suppose, my young brother, that our Castle would impose anything on you that you would scruple to perform on the grounds you mention? Most certainly you can not. But at the same time you must keep in view your duty to your country, and remember that you can not serve your God more acceptably than by heartily espousing the cause of this bleeding land against the encroachments of tyrants."

"Sound," said the Judge.

If he had said "sound and fury," it would have hit the center.

That white-haired old man, who had stood up before the people for half a century, as the chosen servant of Christ, was an arrant hypocrite! I knew it from that moment; and I have it to add that the clergyman, whether North or South, who believes and advocates sentiments like the above, is a living scandal to his profession! I evaded a direct answer, and said:

"We are all at sea in this matter, till we have become familiar with the contents of our packets; and, as an opportunity will soon occur, to know what our Castle wishes and expects as the result of this journey, is it not advisable to defer argument till we know what points for speculation or analysis the subject may present?"

"Sound again," said the Judge. "And that reminds me that our conference is too public for any good to arise from it. Let us defer matters till morning, and we shall then see more clearly what action to take."

We soon landed, and found a hotel with pleasant accommodations. My companions applied for a double-bedded room, it seemed to me, with uncalled-for anxiety and evident nervousness; and there was a manner about them that showed a desire for exclusiveness, and looked like leaving me out in the cold. All of which I noticed incidentally, and thought of at the moment as rather eccentric or whimsical; but had no idea these acts were part of a plan that was studiously arranged before leaving home, to be systematically carried into practice through the execution of our commission. I learned such to be the case soon enough; and further knowledge followed in due order, that taught me deeper lessons in finesse and duplicity than I ever thought it possible to learn.

My friends were provided for according to their wish. A comfortable apartment was allotted to me, in which I had my luggage stowed, and everything made snug, and then went to supper. Particulars of this kind are, doubtless, tiresome; but they all seem necessary to explain fully what follows. On returning to my room, I resolved to study my instructions before retiring, as it was my intention to proceed at once with the business of my appointment. I therefore procured a light, and was about opening the hieroglyphic budget, when my eyes fell on a note, that was lying on my table, addressed to me in an unfamiliar hand, and superscribed "immediate." It was sealed with wax that bore the impress of the snake in a circle, enclosing the crescent and stars, which at once led me to suppose it a document of official character, and doubtless relating to the business in hand. Imagine my surprise when I had opened it and read the following:

"*Dear Sir:*

"Your friend, the Judge, was correct when "it occurred to him that there are men in Galveston *almost* as smart as some of your common people at Augustine," and that "if you get a-head of them, it will be more good luck than superior wit that should have the credit." Let us tell you that yourself and the Judge and the Parson, *are* here on a fool's errand, and did we not consider you perfect damned fools, incapable of effecting a single step toward the vandalism you meditate, you would never have set foot on the soil of Texas; and, further, that if you officiously meddle with affairs here, that you assume to have control over, your quarters will be *permanently* transferred to the dungeon of the Temple, for the term of your natural lives, which term may be long or short, as it pleases . THE TRIUMVIRS."

Here, then, was our welcome to the generous hospitalities of the Lone Star! We, the chosen spies of a great order, had been dogged to the scene of our anticipated triumph, watched like thieves, and before having an opportunity to test our inquisitive or penetrating qualities, threatened like pirates. "The Triumvirs" of Galveston had evidently looked for our coming, and had either gone themselves, or sent out deputies, to meet us. And we had been met, singled out of the crowd of passengers, as "perfect damned fools," and our words listened to and reported in the most approved style of eminent detectives. "O, that there were some one here to write me down an ass!"

I re-read the note, scanned the chirography, lighted a cigar and rang the bell.

"Ring, sah?" inquired the boy at the door.

"I wish to know who brought this note. Can you tell?"

"Eh? Yer mean dat letter? Boy bring him to Mas'r, an' mas'r send him up"

"Ask your master to come to my room."

"Eh? Yes'r! But mas'r kin't come, kaise he's gwine wid de Cunnel, an' Cunnel's waitin'. Missus do, nor Missy Clarey?"

"If your master has not yet gone, ask him to step here a moment. If he is out to-night, I must wait till morning."

"Eh? Yes'r! Dat all?"

"That's all, now. Hurry up before he is gone."

"Yes'r!"

But the boy was too late. Our landlord had gone "wid de cunnel," and I was forced to wait till morning before interrogating him. I therefore consoled myself with translating my budget and weighing its contents, which was work enough for one night; for of all the outlandish characters ever introduced to convey ideas on paper, this cipher was entitled to eminence for its uncouthness and lack of systematic arrangement. But I finally made a point, and found that the first clause was a command that I should not recognize any of the Galveston Knights till I had become fully assured of their status, and learned that they were orthodox; and, under the severest penalties, I was ordered to abstain from visiting a Castle till I was fully satisfied it still adhered to the regular work of the order without interpolation. How I was to make these discoveries was not clear, as no directions were given to that end, except that I should be vigilant, secretive and faithful, and immediately report everything I might discover of a suspicious or unusual character at the scene of our operations. It was therefore in my power to report at once, for something of a suspicious and unusual character had already happened in the circumstance of "The Triumvirs'" note. I laid aside the instructions, and on the spur of the moment transcribed this singular missive, with the circumstances attending its delivery, and addressed the document to the G. K. at San Augustine. Then, in order to insure its immediate transmission, I resolved to carry it myself to the postoffice. I found the walk somewhat tedious, and was at length under the impression I had missed the direct course; therefore stopped at a saloon to inquire.

"The postoffice?" responded a gentleman standing in a crowd near the door; "it is some little distance yet, but I am going there, and have my carriage in waiting. Do me the favor to bear me company."

I readily consented, and seated myself in the vehicle without ceremony.

" You are probably a stranger in town ?" queried my companion.

" Yes ; here less than two hours, and my first visit."

" Little wonder that you have not learned localities. Do you remain long with us ?"

" I think not. A matter of business only, that will probably be soon over—the sooner the better."

We were riding at a good rate of speed, and it was a matter of much surprise to me that we did not reach the postoffice. At length we turned down an alley or by-street, just wide enough for our passage, and I said to my companion,

" Surely, your postoffice is not in such a place as this ?"

" We will soon be there," he replied.

A few steps further on we halted before a heavy door, that looked like the basement entrance of an immense warehouse. All was dark and gloomy, silent and deserted.

" John," said the stranger, addressing his driver, " rap three times on the door with the butt of your whip, and we'll see if there's any one here."

The door was immediately opened, in response to the raps, and a voice from within inquired,

" Who's there ?"

" A pledge of the Three," replied my companion.

In an instant two men came rushing out, and before I was aware of their intention, enveloped my head with a heavy blanket, secured my arms behind with handcuffs, and lifted me bodily from the carriage. I was faint and confused, but had no doubt as to whose hands I was in and for what purpose. Suddenly I experienced the sensation of being borne rapidly along on a litter, and after a little I felt the damp and noisome air of subterranean passages, and heard water drippings and dead echoes like those we hear in caves. Still I was borne on through winding labyrinths, in darkness and silence—no sound save the drippings and the footfalls of my bearers—on through dangerous and secret haunts of men-devils, with unremitting force—on, on ! Finally we reach a circle, and go round and round, faster and faster, in a great whirl, till the bearers are tired and panting, and a grum voice commands,

" Stop !"

The suddenness of the halt threw me from the litter with great force. I was immediately seized and the blanket torn from my head, but found myself in utter darkness, and fearful of making the least motion, lest I might voluntarily inflict an injury on myself. Lying here some fifteen minutes gave me time to reflect, and I soon arrived at the conclusion that I was either in the dungeon of the Galveston Castle, or the stronghold of pirates, and it really mattered little to me which. But if I had any doubts as to whether I was in charge of the brotherhood of the Circle, they were soon dispelled. The booming of a muffled bell grated on my ears, a yell as from all the fiends of pandemonium sounded in response, and a light of more intense brilliancy than would be emitted from a thousand jets burst on my startled vision. Drums rolled and bugles sounded; then came the echo of armed heels and the rattling of sabers. Soon appeared two hundred Knights in splendid armor, with helmets of a strange fashion, ornamented with silver crescents on the fronts and golden serpents couchant on the crowns. They were led by three Knights in black, who wore red feathers in their helmets; and here, at a glance, I intuitively recognized " The Triumvirs " and the " Knights of the Red Rose " as identical.

The Knights ranged themselves around the apartment in silence, the Triumvirs occupying a position in the center.

" Death to traitors !" exclaimed red feather number one.

" Confusion to our enemies !" parroted number two.

" Torture and death to spies !" howled number three.

" So say we all !" responded the knights in unison.

I saw the drift of this mummery and was mad.

" To the devil with renegades and interlopers !" I shouted, and the echoes rang all the changes on the words, like a mighty response.

" Gag his insolence," commanded the foremost red feather, and lead him to our presence.

I was foolish enough to attempt resistance to the execution of this order, but was at once overcome, gagged, and led before the the august Triumvirs. They were standing on a crescent shaped disc, formed of rock, with the mystical triangle in the center, and the letters 3, 7, 5, R, 61, appropriately carved therein.

" Which one ?" inquired the foremost thug, addressing his companion.

" Edmund Wright, of San Augustine, formerly of Atlanta, re-

THE ENEMY ASKS A PARLEY.—See page 135.

ported as giving evidence of unsoundness at the time of his admission into the order, and an inefficient and lukewarm Knight since."

" Why is he here ? "

" He is sent from Augustine as a spy against the brotherhood of Galveston, and to correct what are called our irregularities. He is under special instructions."

" What is the nature of those instructions ? "

" I have them here," said the scoundrel, with unsurpassed effrontery ; "but as they are in an unusual cipher, I will give you the substance in plain English. He is first commanded not to associate with, nor recognize the brotherhood of Galveston, nor under any circumstances to visit our Castle. (He will have a funny report to make under this head, I'm thinking, if he ever reports at all ! ") Next, he is instructed to find all the *true* Knights we have left in this region, and learn from them who first introduced irregularities into the work, and how far these irregularities are sanctioned by the order in Texas. Also, what the interpolations consist of, and how far they interfere with the original objects of the association, as understood by the *great men at Augustine*. Finally, he is authorized to form any combination in his power to regulate our work by force ; if thought necessary, by the shedding of blood and the sacrifice of life."

" But he was not expected to accomplish all this alone ? "

" Oh, no ! He has two companions in this great revolutionary mission, who come with the same objects, from the same source, although their instructions are not identical ; for, while *brother* Wright is smelling out the game here, and watching it, Parson Taylor and Judge Firman are deputed to watch *him*, and see that he is not converted to the heresies that possess us. His master has more confidence in his inquisitiveness than in his virtue, and values his smelling qualities so highly that he will run no risk of losing them."

" Where are the others? "

" *Under the pump !* "

" Are you sure? "

" We never mistake."

" Wright ! this is truly a bad business," said the foremost red feather. " But you see we are prompt to deal with all such eavesdroppers as yourself and your friends. " Under the pump," means that they, as well as yourself, are now in our power, and in this our stronghold.   It is little more than two hours since you arrived in our city, thinking, perhaps, that no one here understood the object of your mission.   This meeting was summoned in ten minutes after you set foot on our soil; and in less than a half hour from that time, a description of your person and that of your companions, was in possession of every Galveston Knight.   You can say, in your report, that we are vigilant—proof against surprise—and firm in our determination to maintain our rights, at all hazzards. That your report may not lack anything, and be full to the last particular, we now propose to initiate you and your two companions into this, our Castle, and you will thus learn all you came to find out, and much more than has been dreamed of by the circumbendibus fogies at Augustine.   Remove the gag and hand-cuffs from the prisoner."

My hands and mouth were soon at liberty, and I was encircled by a guard of eight Knights with drawn swords.   The remaining Knights were formed in column by platoons of sevens, and, at the order of the Chief of the Three, made one grand evolution around the cavern, while myself and my supporters occupied the center. We were ordered to fall in at the rear, and then came the signal, by four taps of the muffled bell; the bugles responded with several eccentric flourishes dying away like the wail of despair; and then came the command:

"March by the Crescent!"

Time was marked by the monotonous tapping of a muffled drum, and we advanced through a semi-circular passage, paved with brick, but the walls of which were of heaviest masonry.   Soon we were passing grated doors of heavy iron; and, as I came opposite one that appeared larger and stronger than the others, we were ordered to halt.   I looked up to the grate mechanically, but what were my sensations to behold there, pressed against the bars, with eyes protruding, in wild affright, the pale face of my fellow-detective, Judge Firman?

CHAPTER IX

A JUDGE Brought to Judgment—He Quails Not—Ruse of the Parson—Extraordinary Harangue of the Triumvir Chief—The Lone Star on her Dignity—Galveston not Augustine—The Great Room of the Temple—"Let the Craven Three Approach"—Decree of the Soldan—The Judge All Spunk—He Disappears.

How the Judge could have been kidnapped and immured in that subterranean dungeon, without my knowledge, was the problem that at once distracted my attention from my own personal beleaguerment. Less than three hours before, he and I and Parson Taylor were sailing up Galveston Bay, intent on the objects of our great mission, and now—

"Bring forth the learned Judge, and place him under a strong guard," commanded Chief of the Three.

The door was unlocked, and the poor Judge seized and dragged out with as little ceremony as would be used in handling a beast. He was brought to his feet with a vigorous jerk that made his teeth chatter. He had been treated with the greatest respect by every one with whom he had come in contact in the last forty years, and now indignities were heaped upon him as though he were the veriest knave in christendom. It was too much for human nature!

He gazed about him for a moment like one bewildered, and then, evidently taking in the whole situation at a glance, he shouted:

"So we have indeed fallen among thieves! Well, scoundrels, do your will. Murder the old man at once, if it suits you. Kill quickly and decently, if you know how; for this pulling, and dragging, and bruising torture, is beneath the dignity of a vulgar pirate. But, remember—with whatever measure ye meet, thus shall it be meted to you again!"

"Stop the old devil's preaching, or shortern his breath at once!" commanded Chief of the Three. "Forward!"

We were soon halted at the door of another dungeon, from which the sounds of groans and sobs came to our ears with special unction. The massive bolts were drawn, and a guard led forth my Christian friend, the fighting itinerant. He was in great disorder, and shaking with an ague of fear, but at once found language for the occasion.

"My friends," said he, "I fully appreciate your feelings, and, if I know my own heart, sympathise with the great object of this convocation. I feel that I can join heart and hand in the business of this important meeting; and, although personally a stranger to most of you, offer my knighthood to the test of any proof you may designate."

"It shall be gallantly tested, old man," responded the Chief of the Triumvirate. "You shall cross the Pons Assinorum with a pasteboard buckler and a dagger of lath—your canteen filled with sweetened whisky, plenty of gingerbread in your haversack, and a smelling bottle at a convenient reach. But none of your Augustine praying and preaching, you old cuss! Save that for a better market."

"Just as your honors wish," said the Parson.

"Honors! my God!" exclaimed Judge Firman; "I have heard of honor among thieves, but—"

"Kill that old reprobate if he utters another word," shouted the Chief. "Forward to Council."

Again we were on the march. At the end of the long corridor there was a wide space, in which the head of the column wheeled, and once more we traversed the semi-circular passage, keeping time to the same dull echoes of the muffled drum. Again we marched through the great cavern to the sound of clanging bugles, and came to a halt around the crescented disk, in the same order as previously described. The Three again occupied the platform; the Chief commanded silence, and then, in tone and manner that made a deep impression, pronounced the most extraordinary harangue I ever listened to, as near as I can remember in the following words:

"Companions of the Circle: We are met for no common purpose. We are here for no ordinary duty. We are summoned for a great object; to meet one of the most critical emergencies that could possibly threaten our Order; and I trust we fully appreciate the occasion, and that we are ready to adopt such measures to avert the impending danger as will be efficient to that end. Spies are sent here to circumvent our plans, betray our confidences, and deliver us over to those who would destroy us! In fact, they come with instructions to array our own people against us, and inaugurate civil war on this soil that shall stain it with our blood, unless we consent to their dictation, and abandon our cherished institutions at their will. Are we, Knights of the Lone Star, ready to submit to these foul indignities? Are we fallen so low that we will impassively consent to become the slaves and minions of Florida, or of any other state or nation? In short, are we the poor fools of others' whims, to be knocked about as the shuttlecocks of their caprices; or are we still men, freemen, with sacred rights dearer than life, and strength to maintain them, or courage to die in their defense?

"Brave Texans! I know your hearts; your indomitable prowess and invincible courage! You are not here to surrender rights, but to reassert and maintain them, at any hazard. You are not here to tamper with and excuse treachery, but, I trust, to make such an example of it as shall leave a *crimson mark on the record of this night's history!* We have apprehended these spies; they are fully in our power, unknown to the civil authorities; their punishment is solely for our determination, for we may work our will with them to the *last result*, without fear of question. For myself, I hope they may never see the light of another sun, and that we may hereafter be able to point to their fate as the great example of our vengeance.

"Do not understand me as wishing to dictate. I have no settled plan for the execution of the judgment I would pronounce, if left to my individual decision, and therefore hope to be favored with the views of my brother Knights, before we determine fully the measure and manner of punishment."

The Chief took his seat, and his Right Bower of the Black Suit stepped forward.

"Knights!" said he, "I never trouble you with long speeches; but I think it right these men be heard in their own defense before we adjudge them. It is just possible we don't know all the points, and it strikes me they havn't the appearance of the worst scoundrels in the world. I hope they may be heard."

"Let them speak!" "Let's hear what they will say!" "Come,

sneaks! spin your yarn!" and similar expressions up and down the column. The Chief came forward hurriedly.

"We can not hear them," said he; "for they have *no right of speech* till they have 'seen what we have seen, heard what we have heard, and know us as we know each other.' If such is your intention, let it be indicated."

The affirmative sign, hands raised with palm turned out, was unanimous.

"Then shall the evesdroppers take their first step this night in the rudiments of Chivalry; and, mind you, Galveston is not Augustine; knighthood here is not the pastime of a leisure hour, but the business of earnest men, into which they carry their hearts, and lives, and *all* they have. There is no indecision nor hesitation here; no recusancy; no opportunity to go back or look back, unless you desire a short journey to hell! It is decided that you take our degrees: you have no power to object, unless you purchase it with every drop of your blood! The issues are now plainly before you. To the great room of the Temple; form column; forward."

Another grand flourish of bugles, three strokes of the great bell, and the muffled drum resumed its measured beat. Once more around the cavern, and then great doors opened at the side, disclosing an immense staircase, rich in all the appointments of luxury, and ornamented with a thousand fantastic gewgaws of mystical design. The insignia of the order was pictured and carved in every conceivable style, and hundreds of objects, of weird signification, now for the first time met my view. The great candelabrum was surmounted by fifteen ghastly skulls, from each of which projected three strangely modeled jets, representing great eyes, and so constructed that they had the appearance of glaring at the beholder like an enraged beast. The handrails represented huge serpents, elaborately gilded; the stairrods were bronzed copperheads; the wainscoting was replete with carvings of grinning skulls and hideous images, among which I remember an odd caricature of a gigantic negro, in the act of putting the knife to the throat of a helpless infant! The falls of several of the steps were brilliant transparencies, with figurative designs, the uppermost of which displayed the words, "Death to Abolitionists."

The Knights marched up these stairs, and were halted on a broad landing from which other stairs led, in different directions, to the rooms above. The drum was silenced; the column formed a hol-

SCENE ON THE TOMBIGBEE.

8

low square, in the center of which myself and companions were placed. The great bell tolled three times; the lights were dimmed to a degree that gave a sombrous look to the entire scene. Thus, all was in immovable silence, for perhaps five minutes; and an ecstasy of nervousness crept through my veins and into my heart as that silence was broken by the voice of a fearful shape that arose in gigantic form through the floor of the second landing, and, in hoarse tones, thundered the command:

"Let the craven three approach!"

"Firman, Wright and Taylor, obey the order of the Soldan of the Temple!" said the chief.

But Firman, Wright and Taylor were spell-bound. The shape was too devilish and frightful to inspire our confidence, and its voice was by no means winning.

"Guards, lead forward!" shouted the chief.

So we were led forward up the steps, and into the immediate presence of the "Soldan."

"False-hearted knaves!" growled he, "why move so slowly at my bidding? But still, 'tis well you fear. Your doom is not calculated to set well on weak stomachs, and blood like yours will soon cool when the air strikes it. Ho!" he shouted, "Nubians, to your work!"

A heavy panel in the staircase was drawn aside at this summons, and six beings, representing large and muscular negroes, stepped out on the landing. They seized us roughly, two to each man, and hurried us, with great violence, through the opening from whence they came.

We found ourselves in what appeared, by the dim light, to be a small apartment; but before we had opportunity for further observation, our eyes were bandaged, our hands tied, and each of us forced down and secured in a strangely oscillating chair, that rolled and jerked in a manner most distressingly eccentric.

"God have mercy on my soul!" groaned Parson Taylor, in great agony.

"Pray rather for mercy on your body just now," said the judge; "and thank God that these hell-hounds can not bind and torture your soul."

"Silence!" thundered the voice of the "Soldan," "or we'll bind and torture your tongues."

The great bell tolled again, and as its last echo reverberated through the caverns and vaults, the chairs in which we were seated began to ascend—at first slowly, and then gradually increasing their speed, until the swiftness of the motion became painful. Still we ascended, or, at least, such was the effect on our senses—up, up, interminably. It was the most singular illusion I ever experienced, and which I shall, probably, never be able to explain; for when I imagined myself far above the clouds, and riding with the stars, I heard the voice of the shape command:

"Let them drop!"

The chairs turned over, the fastenings that held us were unloosed, and we fell, not to exceed ten feet, into a pile of soft cotton.

"Damn such nonsense as this!" shouted the judge, springing to his feet. "I would sooner be killed outright than tortured to death. So do your worst, you cursed devils!"

"Remove all the bandages," said the Soldan, "and summon an armed guard."

When my eyes were at liberty, I found myself in a spacious hall, of great magnificence, furnished in all the splendor that wealth can command. Compared with the temples of other castles I had seen, it was the sumptuous palace beside the plebeian cot.

The guard came in, armed with rifles. They were a set of rough customers, with murder written all over their faces, and seemed to enjoy the prospect of a row.

"Seize the old man!" (pointing to the judge) said the Soldan to the guard, "and place him under the inquisitorial arch. Then three of you, one at each side, and one behind him, with your pieces properly loaded, cocked and in order; press the muzzles firmly against his head, ready to blow his brains out at the signal from me. We find it our duty to make an example of him, for he persists in defying us, and sets our power at naught."

"I do not acknowledge myself as, in any degree, under your authority," replied the judge. "And I hereby not only protest against the force you now propose to use, but against all you have used, and your insolent assumptions in the case of myself and my companions, from the commencement."

"Insolent assumptions, old man? Those words shall cost you dear. Remove him at once to the arch, and, in addition to my first order, place the iron collar about his neck, and arrange the trough to catch his rebellious blood. Away with him!" shouted the

Soldan, in a very agony of wrath; "and, Nubians, bring in your charge these other two, that they may see fair play, and the fore-shadowing of their own fate, under a similar provocation."

Four strong men had fallen upon the poor old Judge, and were binding his limbs with strong cords. This accomplished, they picked him up bodily, and arrayed themselves as the advance of the column. The Parson and myself were placed next, under guard; and a great concourse of Knights came after. As we started, the great bell commenced its muffled toll, and continued while we marched three times around the Temple. Then the lights were dimmed, an immense tapestry, at one end of the room, rolled up, as if by magic, and in a deep recess, or ante-chamber, we beheld the Soldan seated on an elevated throne, clothed in rich garments, and wearing a crown upon his head, sparkling with jewels. In front of the throne appeared a low platform, upon which Judge Firman was placed, in a sitting posture, while myself and the Parson were allowed to occupy chairs at either side. At a signal from the throne, the platform commenced rising, and we then discovered that the Judge was seated on the capital of a richly modeled column, that rose through the floor, and bore him aloft with a gentle motion. We also noticed, in following the motion of the shaft, that there was an aperture in the ceiling of the room directly in line with it, sufficient to admit its passage into rooms above; and were therefore not taken by surprise when the Judge passed through this opening, and was shut out from our view. But in another moment the column descended to its first position, and the platform was empty!

CHAPTER X.

" THE Souvenir of Treachery "—The Judge returns with a tight-fitting Collar—
Firmness not to be Intimidated—The Parson Quavers—The Five Signals—
"Traitor's Doom"—Villainy Triumphs over Nobility of Soul—Massacre
of the Judge—Resolution of the Author—He Vows Retribution and Bides
His Time.

AFTER a brief interval, during which absolute silence was pre-
served, four men, dressed in white robes, with red sashes and tur-
baned, came through a small door, at the rear of the throne, bearing a blood-stained trough. This they placed beside the platform
or top of the column, and returning, soon appeared with a large
black coffin, on which was inscribed, in silver letters, " The Souvenir of Treachery."   This was placed across the backs of two
chairs, between the platform and the throne.

" Guards ! " said the Soldan, " remember your orders, and ob-
serve the signal. Do your duty like true Knights, and all will be
well. Lower the arch."

Again the bell tolled mournfully; but its tones were insufficient
to drown an agonizing shriek that pealed upon us like a wail of
despair, and chilled our hearts. The Judge was returning, suspended by an iron collar about his neck, which depended from the
center of an arch, upon which was painted, in red characters, " The
Traitor's Doom !" This arrangement was lowered by a cable,
attached to machinery above; and as it came slowly down, with an
unsteady, irregular motion, the groans of the poor old man were
pitiful enough to soften a heart of adamant.

" Kill me at once ! for Christ's sake, kill me !" he prayed. " This
torture is more than I can endure."

The collar was not intended to strangle, nor was it considered
extremely severe in a majority of cases; but the corpulency of

Judge Firman made an immense strain on his neck, and the wonder is that it did not break it. His feet soon touched the platform, however, and then his groans ceased; but he was only fairly at a true perpendicular when three of the armed guards stepped forward and pressed the muzzles of their rifles hard against his head.

"Old man," said the Soldan, "do not, for a moment, deceive yourself with the idea that we are playing with your feelings, or endeavoring, by this ceremony, to intimidate your courage. But understand at once that we are earnestly at work, in the performance of a solemn duty, from which nothing on earth, nor in heaven or hell shall deter us. You are required, without prelude or argument, to instantly resign and abjure your commission from San Augustine Castle, appointing you a spy upon the doings of our Order in Texas, and to bind yourself by a solemn oath, under the heaviest penalties, to report nothing you have or may witness here to-night, or elsewhere in Galveston. Your companions will be similarly bound; and then you will be instructed in such of our mysteries as we find it necessary to impart, to hold our authority over you when you go hence; for after you leave us you will still remain under our control as completely as you are at this moment, with the collar about your neck and loaded rifles pointed at your brain!"

"Never, so help me God! will I submit to such tyranny!" exclaimed the Judge. "Torture me if you will—kill me if you dare—for I will not assent to one of your requirements!"

"Have a care, old man! On a very slight signal from me those rifles will divorce your miserable soul from that ugly carcase, and send you to the devil with many sins unrepented of. Have a care!"

"I have no care in the matter, but defy you!" replied the Judge. "I scorn your assumed authority, and none of your threats shall intimidate me."

"Then, sir, we have but one course. You have been warned, and the consequences be upon your own head. Guards, are your pieces all properly loaded?"

"They are."

"A bullet in each one?"

"Yes."

" Pricked and capped ?"

" All complete."

" Are they cocked ?"

" All ready."

" Are the muzzles firmly held against the prisoner's head ?"

" They are."

" You see, sir, that everything is in order, and you have but one minute to live, unless you resign and abjure your commission, and consent to be directed by me."

" Consent at once, man !" cried Parson Taylor.

" Never !" shouted the Judge, firmly. " I will die a thousand deaths first !"

" Well, old man, here is your last chance," said the Soldan. " My hand is now on a bell cord, which I have just pulled once. I shall pull at regular intervals, and at the fifth ringing the guard will certainly fire, unless you retract. Be wise in time, and do not imagine that any one will mistake stubbornness for courage."

" You have my decision ; proceed to your devil's work !" replied the Judge, in firm tones.

" I have now rung the second signal," said the Soldan.

" Judge Firman, are you demented ?" shouted the Parson. " Remember your family and friends at home ; your estate, and all your ties."

" And my HONOR, Parson Taylor ; don't forget that," replied the Judge, proudly.

" What can be done ?" queried the Parson, gloomily.

" I am ringing for the third time," said the Soldan.

" May I be permitted to have one word with my friend ?" asked the Parson."

" There is little time for words now," answered the Soldan; " but from your seat you may address him on the subject before us, in any manner that will not interfere with the execution of his punishment."

" I have no wish to hear from you further, friend Taylor, for I know what you would say," said the Judge. " Remember me to my family and friends, and tell them my death will be no stain on their love or friendship for the old man."

" This is the fourth signal," said the Soldan, " and I can assure you that I am as determined in this matter as you can be. Unless you retract at once your soul is within one minute of eternity !"

CHIVALRY "DOING GOOD BY STEALTH."

"Good by, Taylor; good by, Wright," faltered the old man. "Tell them I died like a man."

"I fear, your honor," said I, addressing the Soldan, "that Judge Firman does not correctly apprehend his own position, or the force of your requirements. Is there not some way you can make the matter more clear to him?"

"I understand your motives, young man, and appreciate them. The time for explanations has passed. Yourself and friend must change your position farther back."

We obeyed ot once.

"Knights," said the Soldan, "this is the *third time* in the history of this Castle that we have been called to look upon a scene like this. Let its lessons sink deep into all our hearts, that we may never forget 'The Traitor's Doom.' The time has come for the final signal. Let there be no faltering, no faintheartedness, no womanly tremors. My hand is now on the cord. Is all ready?"

"All ready," replied the Chief of the Three.

"Unhappy man, may God have mercy on your soul!"

"Amen!" responded all the Knights in unison.

The bugles sounded, the great bell tolled, and the Soldan pulled the fatal cord.

"Fire!"

The rifles were so promptly discharged, at the word of command, that but one report was heard. When the smoke cleared away, the mangled head of the poor old Judge was discovered leaning to one side, motionless in death! The iron collar was unloosed, the black coffin opened, and all that remained on earth of a brave-hearted man deposited therein. The Nubians were ordered to wash the blood from his face; and then the Knights formed column, placing myself and the Parson in the rear, still under guard, and to the measured time of the muffled drums, we were marched around the coffin, to take a last look at the dead. As we gazed upon his lifeless countenance, the Knights constantly repeated the words,

"Behold the Traitor's Doom!"

As I gazed upon the lifeless countenance of that brave old hero, who, although mistaken in many of his judgments, was a *true man*, I resolved that when I should succeed in again reaching the land of civilized men, I would make known to them the horrors I had witnessed under the rule of this terrible oligarchy of the Circle and, although my descriptions are imperfect, and fall far short of the reality, I hope they will open the eyes of the people to an appreciation of the great fact that we have an Order in our land that glories in the perpetration of such deeds of darkness. And it is now my earnest prayer that these fiends may soon be ferreted out, both at the North and the South, and that we may then behold a punishment that shall be truly the "Traitor's Doom!"

CHAPTER XI.

THE Milk in the Cocoanut—The Parson and Author in Better Lodgings— Opportune Discovery of Crinoline and Accompaniments—Hypocrisy— The Parson Emigrates to the Land of Nod—A Clerical Vail Available in an Emergency—Somnolent Guards—Crinoline Challenged—"Who Goes There?"

IT was decided there was not sufficient time for further business, as the night was far spent, and the brethren considerably exhausted. A question was at once started, however, what disposition should be made of myself and Parson Taylor, that we might be on hand for the meeting of the succeeding night. It was suggested by some that we be confined in the dungeon of the Temple; but others proposed that there would be no danger in allowing us to go to the hotel, with an efficient guard, as the landlord would exercise the utmost vigilance for our safe keeping.

"That I will," responded a burly Knight. "If they are not forthcoming when wanted, I agree to fill their places."

Here was the explanation of a portion of the milk in the cocoanut, and I understood where mars' went "wid de cunnel." Also, how our cipher had been transferred to the possession of Galveston Castle. But I preferred returning to the hotel, for many reasons; one of which was that I liked its accommodations better than those of a dungeon, and another, that I did not intend to be present at another session of the Castle, if it was avoidable. A guard of six men was detailed, and permission given us to return to our lodgings.

I asked if we might be permitted to take charge of the remains of Judge Firman, and forward them to his friends for burial.

"The remains of Judge Firman will be buried at once, within these walls," replied the Soldan, "and no one who has not been here to-night will know his fate. You will know our reasons for this before we are through with you, and you will never mention the circumstances you have just witnessed, under pain of a similar fate. You will understand these matters better when we meet again."

The Parson and I were then blindfolded and led away by the guard. We traversed long passages and many large rooms, and I finally knew, by the change of air, that we were once more outside of that thieves' stronghold, and breathing a purer atmosphere. But we were forced to travel a great distance with our eyes covered, and not till we were within a single square of the hotel were the bandages removed. My baggage was ordered into the double room that had been at first engaged by the Judge and Parson, and then commenced a thorough overhauling and diligent search by our guard. They found nothing of a suspicious character, and after appropriating a few articles that seemed to strike their fancy, gave the balance back to our possession. We were informed that the door and windows of our room would be securely fastened, and a strong force posted around the house, so that every chance of escape was cut off. We were allowed the privacy of the room, however, and after attending to the security of the windows, the guard withdrew. I knew that we were watched from a distance, and that any conversation we might indulge in would be overheard, and therefore said to Brother Taylor that we would talk only on the most ordinary subjects, without alluding to our present situation in any manner. We thought it best to retire to bed as though nothing extraordinary had happened, and signified as much to each other by very quiet signs that we understood, but which would not have conveyed a very intelligible idea to an ordinary observer. Necessity is a great sharpener of the wits.

I commenced disrobing at once, and as I opened the wardrobe to hang up my clothing, I espied hanging therein a lady's dress and divers other article of female apparel. My plans were formed on the instant. Many times, in my earlier days, had I disguised myself in female dress, and passed myself off among intimate acquaintances as the anonymous heroine of a score of madcap adventures. My form, long hair, contour of my face, small feet and hands, were all favorable to the success of the deception, and it required only coolness and address to extricate myself from present difficulties, provided the dress was of proper dimensions, and I could find all the little accompaniments that constitute the nameless graces of a feminine outfit. It occurred to me that it would be folly to acquaint my companion with my discovery or designs, as it would be impossible to make him a party to the adventure; and, in fact, I felt no compunctions at leaving him, for I had discovered that he would make way with the Galveston Knights, and agree to everything they imposed, without compromises of honor or conscience. It was near morning. Parson Taylor was very tired, and probably would soon sleep. I therefore dispatched my undressing, and was quickly in bed.

"As we are expected to attend another meeting of the Castle to-morrow night," said I, in a loud tone, "it is best we get what rest we can. I have no idea, however, that we will be called upon to undergo as much labor as we have to-night; for I see nothing extremely objectionable in the requirements of the Soldan, and I am fully determined to comply with his wishes, *when we meet again!*"

"Just my view of the matter," responded the Parson, "and I am truly rejoiced to find that we agree. Had our lamented friend properly reasoned the subject he would have been with us at this moment; and I shall always believe that he fell a sacrifice to the natural obtuseness of his intellect."

O, Hypocrisy! what a goodly outside!

It was nearly an hour before I heard the hard, regular breathing, that assured me the Parson was sound asleep. The house was very quiet. I slipped carefully from the bed, and crept to the door on my hands and knees. With one eye at the keyhole, I discovered a dim light in the hall,—with one ear turned to the same neutral position, I enjoyed the sonorous respirations of a heavy sleeper. I tried the door, gently at first, and then with a little more force, but it would not yield. It was locked, and, without doubt the key was in the pocket of the sleeping guard!

Here was a difficulty I had not counted on, and I was about returning to bed, when it occurred to me to examine the lock more closely. I found, on inspection, that the port into which the bolt was forced, was simply fastened to the door-frame by two ordinary screws, the heads of which projected considerably; and it did not require the extreme stretch of my inventive genius to discover that the blade of my pocket-knife would turn these screws, and allow me to open the door as easily as though it were unlocked.

And now for the wardrobe. As I opened it, I glanced at the window, and saw that day was just dawning. My " maiden " toilet must be hasty, if I would have it effective, and I therefore lost no time in bewailing the fact that I had "nothing to wear." There was all I needed; skirts, hoops, chemise, long white stockings, little gaiter boots, a pink shawl, and one of the jauntiest hats you would find in a whole day's shopping. They fitted so-so, but would have been all right, had I not deemed it prudent to wear my pants and vest underneath, as a reserve, whose services some possible contingency might call into action. I expect the ill-will of my lady readers for this evident profanation, as I can only plead the remarkable exigencies of the occasion in excuse!

As in other days, I rolled my pants up beyond the point where impertinent curiosity would make any unpleasant discoveries; drew on the long stockings of snowy whiteness, and fastened them with the delicate garters; wedged my feet into the little gaiters without accident; donned the hoops, the balmoral and the white skirts; put on the dress, the shawl, the hat, and the gloves; shoved what remained of my masculine apparel up the chimney; and, presto! here I was Hattie Billings, with two rows of buttons down the front, and flounces all around! But I must have a vail, for rouge and alabaster require time and patience, and time was flying rapidly. I searched through the wardrobe, in several bandboxes, and all through the hiding places of the room, but no vail rewarded my labors. I had almost concluded to go without, and "face down" everybody I might meet, when I happened to recollect a large piece of crape on the Parson's hat. I took it without a single twinge of conscience, for I was convinced he wore it as an emblem of sentiments he did not feel; and, although it was a poor substitute for what I wanted, it did me good service in a time of great need.

I lost no time in opening the door, which I effected noiselessly. As I stepped into the hall, I discovered two of the guard lying on the floor, evidently in deep slumber; but as I turned into a darker portion of the passage where the rays of the dim light did not penetrate, I was confronted by a more wakeful sentinel, with piece at shoulder, who challenged me, in a gruff voice, with the query,

"Who goes there?"

THE SPY OF THE HATCHIE.

CHAPTER XII.

MISSY Clary personified — Liberty Regained — Widows plenty in Galveston— Influence of the Almighty Dollar on " Widder Kindercut " — Hoops Discarded in the Land of Dreams—Galveston women not posted as to that fact—Hunger requires no Luxury—Uncalled-for room-mate—Price of an Escaped Prisoner in the Lone Star State.

BEFORE I had time to recover my scattered wits, the accommodating fellow came to my rescue with the remark:

" Oh, it's a woman! Beg parding, mum; but we're here on guard, and have very strict orders; we've nothing to do with women folks; so you may pass along, ef yer like."

I curtesied deeply, and moved forward, thinking it might not become me to utter my thoughts in that company. Tripping down the stairs in all the careless abandon of wild eighteen, I espied another member of the Soldan's special police, in the hall below. He looked up with a startled air, when he heard my step, coolly brought his gun to a line with my head, and commanded:

" Halt! "

The loud, sharp tones of his voice echoed through the house, and I soon heard foot-steps approaching in several directions. My first impulse prompted me to throw myself on the mercy of the man, and trust in Providence for the issue; but, as I was on the point of doing so, a door was opened from one of the lower rooms, and a negro boy entered. He stared at the sentinel, and then looked at me inquiringly. Finally, some idea of the situation found its way through his tangled wool, and he excitedly exclaimed:

" Yer gwine ter kill Missy Clary? Um! better not du dat. Mas'r kill yer, *shore*."

" Jem, is thet thar Missy Clary, true? " queried the guard.

" *Shore*, true, thet am; so, drap yer dam ole shutein' iron, er thar'll be trubbel."

One of the guard at the upper landing now inquired:

" What's the matter with thet woman? "

"Nothin' much," replied the guard of the first floor, "only I halted her ter obey orders. It's Missy Clary, Jem says, so yer kin jist go back an' mind yer own bizness, an' I'll take good kere o' mine. Yer ain't halted no longer, mum," said he to me, "an' I beg parding."

"Haw! haw!" laughed the upper floor guard, "Dick Walsh is growin' monsus sharp. He's 'feered them spies will git away in wimmin's fixins."

I did not wait to hear the continuation of this interesting confab, but unlimbered at once, and proceeded, with a dignified gait, to the main door of the hotel. It was locked and bolted, but the keys were there, and the bolts easily withdrawn. I trembled under an ague of fear, that would have betrayed me, had I been closely watched; but I at last succeeded in making my egress, without accident, and found myself alone, in the streets of Galveston, at liberty to go whithersoever my inclinations tended.

I had no fixed plan, but the idea had in some manner possessed me, that if I could make my situation known to some woman, that had facilities to hide me for a few days, I would be able to escape from the city. The question was, how to find the woman. I walked about for near an hour, revolving this idea in my mind; and when I had arrived at something like a plan, found myself far out in the suburbs, among the negro huts and poorer whites. I knocked at the door of a decent appearing cottage, and was answered by a young lady with a tolerably good-looking countenance and a shabby dress.

"I am looking for a widow lady," said I, "who lives somewhere in this part. I have forgotten her name, but would know if I heard it. Do you know of any widows living hereabout?"

"Widders? golly, yes! Ther's mor'n yer kin shake a stick at. Widder Sutton, she lives over thar," pointing across the street, "an then thar's widder Oliver, and widder Jones, and widder Pullan, an' a thousan' more. Mother's a widder, tu. Is it enny of them?"

"What is your mother's name?"

"Widder Kindercut, mum."

"Ah, that's it," said I, resolved to make a bold push, hit or miss. "Can I see her?"

"'Course yer kin. Walk along!"

I entered the house, and followed the girl to the living room, where I found a woman of about forty-five, engaged in the labors of the household.

"Woman wants ter see yer," was the form of introduction adopted by the girl.

The "widder" glanced at me uneasily, took a black pipe from her lips, and grunted out:

"Take a cheer. Wat yer want?"

"I called, my good woman, to see you on a little matter of business; to accomplish which it seems proper that I consult you alone. Will you favor me with a few moments in private?"

"Wal, reckon it's no use. Sary's all that's har', and yer may say what yer please 'fore her."

"Well, then, I am away from home, on business. I am alone, and do not like to stop at a hotel, unprotected. Hearing that there was a genteel, respectable widow lady living here, I resolved to apply to you for board and lodging while I am in the city, and for which I am willing to pay liberally."

"Dunno. Reckon can't du it. How much'll yer pay?"

"Whatever you think is right, my good woman. Will two dollars a day satisfy you?"

"Tu dollars? Say three, and it's a go!"

"Very well; three dollars it is. I shall want a room by myself, where I can rest from the fatigues of my journey, and where I can remain undisturbed at my leisure."

"Yer kin hev it; but must see ther money fust."

I handed her a ten dollar piece, which proved an efficient "open sesame" to her heart, for she said, with all the politeness she could muster,

"Yer a true lady, *shore*. Walk inter thet thar' room, an' see ef it's sootable. Sary, show ther lady."

I found a comfortable apartment, tolerably furnished, and a very good bed. The bed was tempting, for sleep had not visited my eyelids for more than twenty-four hours. So, telling the girl I would not need breakfast, I dismissed her, slipped off my hoops, fastened the doors, and was in the land of dreams in five minutes.

That was a glorious sleep, and a long repose; for it was late in the day when a sharp rapping at the door awakened me, and the voice of my hostess inquired,

"Arn't yer hungry? Come an' take a bite of somethin' er yer'll starve."

"Soon as I can dress," I answered.

"Laws, Sary,'[2] I heard her say, " ef that thar' woman arn't ondressed !"

I made my toilet, parted my hair in the middle, after a great deal of wetting and combing, admired myself several times in the widow's cracked mirror, and then went to "take a bite of somethin'. " I made a hearty meal of " corn bread and common duins," which was the fare at Hotel Kindercut. I will say, however, that I never partook of a meal with a keener relish, and what was lacking in quality I made up liberally in quantity. The widow was full of pleasant talk, with an occasional joke that sounded just a little coarse from the lips of a female; but she was ignorant of the sex my skirts disguised, and perhaps excusable. I praised her viands, and evidently succeeded in establishing myself firmly in her favor.

The meal over, I again retired to my room, as I thought it advisable to keep as much as possble from view; but the widow soon followed me, and said:

" I guv yer this room 'thout thinkin' ter say that Sary'll hev ter sleep har tu; but reckon yer'll not kere. She'll wash herseff 'fore she goes ter bed, and won't 'sturb yer in ther leas'. She'm a good chile, and reckon yer'll kinder lik' 'er."

What could I say? What could I do? What, under these circumstances, was my duty to myself and to the widow? If I discovered my true character she would turn me adrift. If I carried out my assumed programme I might do her a great wrong. If I objected to her proposition I should offend her, and jeopardize my safety. If I assented to it,—

Well, there was no other course, for nice distinctions could not be considered now; so I said,

" I shall like her, without doubt, and have no objection to your proposal."

" Mabbe ye'd like to go down in ther town. Sary'll go with yer, ef yer like, an' show yer all ther places."

" Not to-night, my good woman; I am too much fatigued. Is there any news to-day?"

" O, yes! I ean 'most forgot. A pris'ner er somthin' got away last night, an' ther's a great noise 'bout it. Ther offer a hundred dollars fer him, dead er alive. God! wouldn't I like ter nab him ?"

" You? O, no! A lady would not desire to engage in such business, I imagine. You only would like to have the hundred dollars. Is not that the point?"

"Sartin'! that's all I'd kere. Ther pris'ner might go where he pleased ef I on'y had ther cash."

The lovely widow then withdrew, and I occupied myself until night with several old newspapers and pamphlets I found in the room. They were the household library.

CHAPTER XIII.

MODESTY severely Tested—Caution comes to the Rescue—Waking Dreams between the Sheets—Proximity of the Sex murders Sleep—Disguised Crinoline in Jeopardy—Galveston Feminines not quite such Fools as they seem
—The Author must needs " cave," and resorts to the Golden Charm—He
makes a Virtue of Necessity, and bargains for a more Masculine Metamor-
phosis.

"ADVERSITY makes us acquainted with strange bedfellows." The
lessons of adversity, properly appreciated, rarely fail to prove of
great benefit to the attentive student; but there is no system of
ethics that furnishes *me* rules for moralizing on the bedfellows.

At an early hour of the gloaming, Sary entered my room, and,
sans ceremonie, commenced divesting herself of her clothing, preparatory to retiring. I am naturally modest, and like to do good
by stealth; I, therefore, very cautiously changed my position,
turned my chair, and seated myself with my back toward her. I
bit my lips with the determination of a Joseph, and indulged in
many severe reflections on the status and general character of Mrs.
Potipher!

The motions of Sary, pattering of her bare feet, rustle of her garments, and general preparation for a *tete-a-tete* with the sleepy god,
kept me awake to her presence; and I soon heard the motion of
the bed covering, the contented sigh at the prospect of grateful repose, and all was suddenly still. She had not spoken a word; and
I had not dared to risk the unsteadiness of my utterance, even in
the presence of that untutored girl; for there is an instinct implanted in every nature that takes alarm from tones and motions,
however much we may seek to counteract their influence by smiles
and fair words.

In a few minutes the heavy respiration of the maiden assured
me she was slumbering, and I therefore concluded to prepare for

my own rest. After examining all the fastenings of the windows and doors, closing the shutters, drawing the curtains close, looking under the bed and in the wardrobe, I relieved myself of crinoline and gaiters, extinguished the light, and deposited myself between the snowy sheets of the widow Kindercut's best shake-down, with a firm trust in Providence. I reclined my weary head on the widow's downy pillows, with a conscientious reliance in the teachings of Plato; and drew the counterpane up under my chin, with a quiet smile at my shivering tremors. It was quiet without, and quiet within, but I did not sleep. In fact, it was several hours before I could sufficiently subdue the nervousness induced by my peculiar situation, to make any respectable advances to "nature's sweet restorer;" and even when I thought myself in proper mood for a comfortable snooze, naughty thoughts *would* creep into my mind and set my brain whirling again.

I finally composed myself in a remarkable degree by repeating the catechism, mentally, and then by sending my thoughts away to distant scenes, and dwelling on the occurrences of past years; but, at last, when all was promising serenity and peace, Sary was suddenly taken with a restless fit, gave a great kick, rolled over plump against me, threw her arms around my neck and exclaimed, passionately:

" Wy, Sam, wus yer har? "

Heigho! I am not sure I slept at all that night. My recollections are sadly mixed and confused; but I do know that, turning my back to Sary, I went to thinking vigorously of the ten commandments, Watts' hymns, and the Constitution of the United States. These exhausted, I wondered what might be doing at San Augustine; what the G. K. would think when he knew the action of the Galveston Castle, and what my wife would think, could she realize my present situation under protection of widow Kindercut. Other things I thought of would fill a volume; what my mind did not run on, is not worth mentioning.

Through all the weary hours of that night, I implored Morpheus in vain — suffering miserably, and knowing it were vain to expect relief. It was by far the longest night I ever experienced, and would make a chapter in Sala's Philosophy Between the Sheets, of absorbing interest. Such a chapter would be out of place here.

Morning came tardily through a dense fog; but with the first peep of dawn I arose, though unrefreshed, and made my hybrid toilet.   I had not taken off the outer dress, and retained under its broad folds my pants and vest, for fear of sudden surprises.   I supposed Sary to be yet asleep, as she was very quiet; but as I was arranging hoops and skirts, in my awkward way, I thought I detected a suppressed giggle from the bed.   Looking around suddenly, I was just in time to catch a glimpse of a head dodging beneath the counterpane.   I said at once:

"Good morning, Sary."

No reply.

"Sary, will you dress and take a walk with me?"

"Eh?" with a sleepy yawn.

"Come! you're not asleep.   Will you dress and take a walk?"

"Reckon not.   Don't want ter git up yit, kaise its tu airly."

"Well, I'm going out, but will return in time for breakfast." ;

It looked as though the jig was up, for the girl had evidently penetrated my disguise, and would lose no time in communicating her discovery to the widow; but I resolved to put on a bold front, and proceed to the carrying out of my plans as circumstances would seem to dictate.   My walk did not extend far, for my anxieties soon compelled me to retrace my steps.   When I returned, the widow met me at the door with many smiles and hearty greetings, and with great cordiality invited me to the morning meal.   Her manner was entirely changed from the previous day, and she was jovial and hearty in the extreme; so much so, in fact, that it seemed affectation.   We were seated around the comfortably furnished table, and then commenced the gossip usual on such occasions, with a fair spicing of the widow's peculiar jokes and boisterous merriment.   At length, with a sudden movement, she turned to me and said abruptly:

"Mabbe I didn' har yer name rightly wen yer fust come; ef I did, I disremembers it."

"Billings, ma'am; I am called Hattie Billings at home."

"Reckon thet's a lie! Yer arn't no woman, but a man, *shore*,— an yer knows it."

"But, my good woman, you do not suppose—"

"No, no! I did'nt say '*spose;* I sed *shore*, an' I say it agin."

"What object do you think I could have in trying to deceive you as to my sex?"

"Ha! ha! thet's the pint! Why, man, yer ther prisn'er, WRIGHT, kaise thet's jist ther rig he stole frum Clary Jen'nins, an' got 'way frum ther guard kaise they 'sposed '*twas* Clary. Ha! ha! thet was dun slick, but yer can't play it outer me, stranger! Sary, lock them doors, an' ef he moves, hit him yer damndest with thet thar poker. We'll hev ther hundred, or blood enuff ter make it squar!"

"Hear me a moment," said I, "and I think you will not con-/ sider it necessary to lock the doors or spill blood. Assuming that I am the person you suppose, and you arrest and hand me over to those who have offered a reward for my apprehension; what then? Do you think they will pay you a hundred dollars? Do you imagine they will give a *woman* credit for so important an arrest? No; but they will at once charge you with hiding me from their search, which I will confirm, and then, instead of obtaining the promised reward, you will be arrested as an accomplice, and be compelled to suffer a long imprisonment. But if you let me make terms with you, all will be well. I will give you a hundred dollars, provided you keep my presence here a secret, and assist me in procuring such disguise, in exchange for this, as shall assist me in eluding the observation of those who are now on my track, till I can escape from the city. I have the money, and will hand it over when you procure me the dress of a countryman, a false beard, and a pair of good revolvers, for all of which I will pay a round price. Now, what say you?"

"Then yer be Wright, sartin! Wal, I 'spect yer a gentleman, an' so I don't mind, pervided yer pays smartly. Yes, Sary an' I'll git ther fixins for yer, I reckon. 'Spose yer wants ter be orf suddent?"

"Soon as possible. In an hour, if arrangements can be completed in that time."

"Wich ther jist can't, but mabbe after dinner it kin be fixed. Ther fixins' yer wants will take a heap o' change, an' yer'd best shell out now. Sary'll go ter town for 'em right away."

I handed the girl some gold, which she took with a strange grimmace, and then donned her hat and left on a run. Her looks and motions did not reassure me, but I had no course but to patiently await the result of her mission, and hope for the best.

CHAPTER XIV.

Suspense—"Widder Kindercut" on the Alert—Down the Cellar—Suspicious
Bundle—Another Disguise Essential to Safety—One Hundred Dollars
Pass Like a Dose of Salts—Kindercut Personified Lowers the Dignity of
Texan Valor—Whisky a Remedial Agent in Desperate Cases—How Sary
Concealed False Whiskers—Capillary Adornments Rather Expensive.

THE widow was very talkative. She wouldnot lose sight of me
for a moment, but when I went into the sleeping room she followed, not more than two paces in the rear, and kept her eyes on
all my motions. She staid there while I staid, and when I returned to the living room, she was still my shadow. Her eyes told
me as easily as her lips could have worded it that she had a
hundred dollars interest in me, and she would take good care of it.
She was doubtless a very prudent manageress.

Thus passed three or four hours, and about noon I began to get
nervous. Although it seemed to me the widow would not neglect
her pecuniary interest, and render it questionable, by betraying
me, of course I did not know what secret motives were lying at
the bottom of her skirmishing; and Sary might, at that moment,
be engaged in bargaining my liberty for a better price than I had
bid. The Kindercuts were evidently shrewd, with all their ignorance; and if they possessed any principles of honor, they doubtless allowed them to lie dormant for more suitable occasions. Still
time passed, and Sary did not come.

"I am afraid some accident has happened the girl," said I.
"She is now at least two hours over the time you fixed."

"Never yer fear. Thet gal 'll come all straight, *shore*; an' she
knows ther best plans for workin' it. Don't be afeerd, not in ther
least."

Another hour passed, and then the widow began to look troubled.
She gazed anxiously from the window, paced the floor rapidly,
puffed at her pipe with uncommon vigor, and gave ample evidence

of extreme nervous excitement. Glancing out the window again, she exclaimed, suddenly,

"Through that door with yer, inter ther celler. Don't make a noise, but be still es a dead man till yer hear from me. Quick now!"

I was in the cellar quick enough, but there was no time to spare before I heard a knocking at the door, and soon the sound of voices in conversation. It was a lengthy *tete a tete*, and evidently interesting, for occasionally I heard the widow's coarse tones pitched high, and her foot brought down heavily, to give emphasis to the text. After a time she opened the cellar door and called,

"Miss Billing, yer kin come up. Thar's summat yer wants to know."

I found a young girl with Madam Kindercut, apparently a dozen years old; and this was her story, divested of idiomatic verbiage:

Sary had arrived at her (the girl's) mother's house at about their dinner hour, pursued by three men, who insisted on examining the contents of a bundle she carried. She told them it was a suit of clothes, and a few other articles, that a shopkeeper in the city was sending to this woman's house, and that she knew nothing regarding the articles, except that she was to leave them there, for which service the shopkeeper had paid her. The men came into the house rudely, took possession of the bundle, examined it thoroughly, inquired as to the exact location of the shopkeeper, and then left. Sary did not dare to take the bundle away—did not like to lose sight of it, and thereupon sent the girl to report progress to her mother and myself. And now the widow wanted to know what was to be done.

I thought a moment.

"Madam," said I, "I have the utmost reliance in your honesty of purpose and the judgment of Sary. I wish now to personate yourself to your child, and, in order to go to her rescue in proper order, wish to exchange this dress for a suit of yours. I will make the change, and accompany this child to her mother's, where, I have no doubt, we shall succeed in outwitting those who are on her track in search of me."

"But they'll nab yer, ef yer go," replied the widow.

"No more than they would you," I replied. "Get me the dress, and see what a splendid widow Kindercut I'll make."

She did as I directed, and I withdrew to my room and made the change. I wrinkled my face with clay and burnt cork, drew a delapidated bonnet over my head, stuck a short pipe between my lips, and hobbled forth.

" 'Clar to grashus!" screamed the old woman, "that thar arn't yer seff? Wal, I'm dun beat, *shore*. Ef I look as nigh ther divil as that, yer may shute me."

And she laughed merrily.

" Do you think I'll pass?"

" *Shore*, true, yer will. Yer'll go through like a dose o' salts."

I felt complimented. Counting a hundred dollars into her ready palm, I said:

" I shall remember you gratefully, and will make such a compensation to Sary for her services as shall fully satisfy you both."

" Jist throw in another ten for luck, now," pleaded the woman.

I was certainly taken aback by her effrontry, but did as she proposed, and said my adieus.

There was plenty of time on the way to instruct my little companion in her role, and, when we arrived, she was fully posted. She went in first to reconnoiter and instruct Sary in the general plan, the principal point of which was to call me " mother," first, last, and all the time, regardless of what might happen. I soon followed, and Sary said:

" 'Spec yer thort I wus lost, mother, but I kin take kere uv myseff yit. Want me ter hum?"

" Wal, no! But wat's ther muss, Sary?" Es ther enny trubbel?"

" Golly! 'pears ter me 'tis mother, *shore*." Then recollecting herself, she added, " ther's a feller comin' down ther road thar, thet'll make trubbel ef he kin. Him an' two other fellers was har, an' looked in ther bundle, an' then went back ter town ter see 'bout it. He'll do some divilment, mabbe, when he gits har."

Sure enough, there he came, with gun across his shoulder, and a military style that seemed to court promotion in every movement. He marched through the gate into the yard, up the steps and into the house, like one having authority.

" Aha, yer little cuss!" said he, as his eyes alighted on Sary; " I'm arter ye, so git yer baggidge and come along. Yer'll hev a sweet time, I reckin, in ther stun jug."

" Jist yer keep still, Sary," said I, " till we find wat all this yar's about. I reckon thar's no great hurry."

"Damn yer, jist talk wen yer hev summat ter say,' responded the fellow, turning sharply on me. "'Spose yer own thet brat, an' mabbe hev brung her up ter steal things frum 'onest folks. Yer kin jist come along tu."

"Oh, mammy!" exclaimed Sary, "now yer air in trubble tu— O, dear? O, dear! wat kin I du?"

"Do as I do. Whoop!" I shouted, at the top of my voice; and falling briskly on the poor frightened devil, I wrenched the rifle from his grasp, and, with a powerful blow, felled him to the floor. Blood flowed profusely, but I lost no time in securing my game, so handsomely grounded, with strong cords about arms and legs. The people about me were in an ecstasy of fear, but obeyed my orders with alacrity, prepared a rude couch for my patient, and furnished me water and restoratives to bring him around again. He soon opened his eyes, and gazed at us with stupid wonder. He did'nt clearly see all the points, so I waited and formed my plans.

In about an hour he asked for a drink of whisky. Convinced that this was sufficient evidence of returning reason, I approached him and said:

"I am sorry to see a man persecuting a little girl, and trying to intimidate unprotected women, because he imagines himself strongest. I apprehend you found your match, this time; and now I have a proposition to make, which you will do well to heed and comply with. I have coat, pants and vest, in this bundle, that I am going to exchange for your's. I shall also borrow your rifle, and such other articles about you that will suit my convenience. These matters you will not report to any one, on pain of treatment similar to that you have just received. You will remain in this house through the night, nor attempt to leave it, on your peril."

"Jist so, old woman. Jist as you say; I don't keer a damn! But, fer God's sake, guv me some whisky."

I poured him out a large drink, which he gulped down greedily, and then arose to a sitting posture.

"Ef yer want them fixins," said he "take 'em, and be damned; but let a feller hev summat ter drink."

I commenced relieving him of his dry goods at once, fearing I had already wasted too much time, conversing in the meanwhile to attract his attention.

"You know I am not a woman," said I; "for a woman never strikes such a blow as you just received."

"Yas; I know well 'nuff. Yer the feller I'd like tu ketch, fer 'twould be wuth jist a clean hunderd; but 'scuse *me* frum ketching enny more jist now."

The exchange of clothing was easily effected, and I retired to another room to array myself in the garb of the wounded man. I wanted his clothes because I knew he *could* describe them, perfectly; and my idea was to wear them away from the house, and manage to exchange them, at the first opportunity, for something entirely different, so that the description of dress, in the hands of my pursuers, would lead my enemies astray till I was beyond their reach. When I returned, I found the man in good spirits, for Sary understood the general features of the plan sufficiently to give him plenty of whisky, and he was whisky-happy with a vengeance. I called Sary aside and asked if she succeeded in finding a false beard. She had, but it was hidden about her person where it was necessary for her to retire to a private apartment to discover; but it was soon in my possession. I then gave her twenty dollars, the same amount to the woman of the house; charged them to let the prisoner go in the morning; shouldered the rifle and sallied forth on my uncertain pilgrimage.

PURSUIT OF THE ANDREWS PATRIOTS—See page 60.

10

CHAPTER XV.

GALVESTON in the background, and Lafitte's Fort the hoped-for Haven of
Safety—The Hand Bill—Short "Shutes" have their Impediments—"Devil's
Hole" prepares for a Siege—Quagmires hold tight—Friendship in the rough
not to be Sneezed at—Booty and Beauty—Rendezvous in the Cactus.

IN an hour I was beyond the corporate limits of Galveston, but
did not think it best to stop till I had placed several miles between
me and the city. I had an indefinite idea of the location of Lafitte's
Fort, and the old rendezvous of his band, on the west shore of the
island; and it was my intention, without any tangible reason why,
to proceed thither, and lie in hiding until the excitement attending
my escape had died away. Night overtook me when I had accomplished about ten miles of the journey, but the breeze from the bay
had dispelled the fog, and the stars twinkled in all their loveliness.
I trudged along briskly, much elated at the success of my plans of
escape, and now convinced that I would outwit my persecutors.
Such is the effect of a fair prospect on a sanguine temperament.

At about nine o'clock I came to a small country inn, and, after
carefully reconnoitering, concluded to stop for refreshments. I
entered and called for supper, which was promised in a short time.
While it was preparing, I sauntered about the public room, reading
the notices of runaway negroes, auction sales, etc., till my eye
caught a small paper, setting forth, in cramped chirography, a description of the person of Edmund Wright, and offering a reward
of one hundred dollars for his apprehension. I became so interested in this paper that I read and re-read it, until the landlord, a
hearty, jovial countryman, came up, slapped me on the shoulder,
and remarked:

"So yer arter the *hundred*, tu? Wal, yer chances air mighty
slim, fer mor'n a dozen hev gone fer it, and not 'nour ago three

fellers stopped, and tuk suthin with me, thet was agoin tu old Lafitte's fort, kaise ther 'spect this Wright cuss hes hid thar. Whar
be yer gwine ter look?"

"I was gwine ter the fort tu," I replied, adopting the vernacular
lingo; "but dunno the road rightly, kaise never was thar."

"Wall, 's no use. Them fellers 'll ketch 'im ef 'es thar; but ef
yer bound ter go thar, I'll guv yer th' shute."

"Ef I don't help, I'll see ther sport, so yer may as well guv me
ther pints."

He therefore gave me full directions. There were two ways of
going, one of which was short, and dangerous, in consequence of
swamps and chapparel; the more lengthy route, a good road, and
the one taken by my pursuers. Of course, I at once decided on
the short "shute" in my mind, but gave my host the impression I
would go the other way.

I ate a good supper, replenished my whisky flask, paid the reckoning, and sallied forth. Keeping the main road for near a mile,
I found the signs indicating the short route, and at once turned to
encounter its uncertain dangers. It was truly the rough way, and
my experience began with the first thirty yards, for I had not proceeded more than this distance when I missed my footing on a log,
and sank to my waist in the miry clay. Had I not clung to some
boughs that were happily within my reach, I would have doubtless
disappeared altogether, for there was no perceptible bottom to the
marsh, and, as they say in those diggings, it was "powerful saft."
The boughs, however, were not of sufficient strength to pull me out,
but merely kept me in position, and I was startled to find that every
effort I made to extricate myself, only caused me to sink lower in
the mire! Keeping quiet as possible, I tried to devise ways and
means to bring myself again to the surface; but the log, the only
substantial foundation of my hopes, was behind me, and I dared not
make the necessary exertion to "face about." My rifle was slung
with a strap across my shoulders, and it seemed that I might detach
it, reach the log, and lift myself by the leverage thus furnished—
and was preparing to execute this plan when I heard the sound of
voices and footsteps approaching from the forest of chapparel. I
quickly examined my piece, cocked it, and prepared to defend my
position; nor were these preparations too promptly made, for just
then the bull's-eye of a dark lantern was turned upon the very spot
I occupied, and a voice exclaimed:

"Lay low, boys! I seen suthin' shine like a rifle bar'l out thar in the Devil's Hole, an' I reckin it means trubble. We oughtn' ter come out this way, an' I know'd it; but now we're har, thar's no use ter turn tail. We'll tarn orf ther glim, an' hail ther innemy."

"Wy, Dave, I didn' see nothink," said another voice. "Mabbe some o' them Galveston chaps air sportin' round, but who keers fer 'em har? We cud lay out twenty o' them chaps, *shore*, so don't git skeert. Ho thar!" he shouted, "who's a hidin' in ther Devil's Hole?"

Convinced they were not my pursuers, and experiencing something like a hankering for their friendly interference, I answered:

"I'm a stranger in these parts, have lost my way, and fell into the swamp, from which I can not release myself without assistance. If you will lend me a hand, I shall be grateful."

"Thet arn't no Galveston chap," said the first speaker, "fer I know that by his patter. Les lend a han', Bill Davis, an' pull him outn' the mud."

Again showing the light, they advanced very cautiously, peering anxiously into the gloom, as though suspicious of an ambuscade. At length they reached the log that had formed the stumbling-block to my progress, and I reached to them the butt of my rifle, firmly grasping the barrel with both hands, in the expectation that they would draw me forth from my uncomfortable imprisonment without delay. But they didn't "take." In a moment I heard them conversing in suppressed whispers, which, by degrees, assumed the form of angry contention.

"Course he's 'n infernel spy," said one. "Arn't sich a d—d fool, I jist arn't, not ter mind thet thar toggery. I say, shute ther cuss on ther spot, an' let 'im bury hisseff a' long es he kin put in ther time!"

"Gentlemen," said I, "my dress may look suspicious, for I had it of a suspicious chap in the city; but for him and *his class* I have no more friendship than you seem to have. Release me from this quagmire—previous to which you may disarm me, if you wish—and if you do not find my words true, my life is at your disposal."

"Wal, I'm d—d ef thet thar arn't reg'lar 'nuff; but ther can't be no foolin'. Ef we finds snakes, we kills em, *shore;* so jist keep yer eye peeled."

They took possession of my rifle, cut a stout pole, and, cautioning me, to loosen my feet as completely as possible from my boots, as the boots were now planted "for keeps," placed one end of the pole on a low stump that happened to be in convenient range, while they held firmly to the other end.

This was the lever of my deliverance; and, grasping it firmly, I exerted my strength to reach *terra firma* at a bound.

I could not move a hair! Had I been impacted in the firmest rock—supposing such a substance to yield to my admission, and shape itself huggingly to my form, it seemed to me I could not be in a more hopeless situation.

The men laughed heartily; and one said,

"Thet won't tally, stranger. Yer can't pull out by no jerks; but yer mus' commince gradooel, an' take it easy, like gittin' married. Eh, Bill?"

"Yas, thet's so. Ef yer got eny whisky, take a swig fust, an' thin commince squirmin' jist lightly. In 'bout three or four hour yer'll come, ef yer kin git out o' yer butes an' stan' ther press!"

My God! three or four hours! I took a liberal draught from my flask, and showed symptons of squirming. In ten minutes the clay was considerably loosened around me, and I was able to turn partially, so that I had one eye on my rescuers.

They encouraged me continually, and engaged in a cheerful conversation that was very effective in keeping up my spirits.

At length, I was enabled to draw one foot from its bootless encumbrance, and soon followed its companion; and then, with a great lift, I was raised bodily from the reeking quag, and landed in all the damp agony of a thorough swamp pickling.

I felt most miserably diluted, and it was quite impossible for me to control my perpendicular for even a moment; so I piled myself on a little collection of boughs that Dave and Bill collected, and, in reply to their questions, related my story of escape from the Thugs of Galveston; not omitting to detail the manner by which I became possessed of the suspicious apparel in which they found me disguised.

I knew, instinctively, that my story would enlist their sympathies, but was hardly prepared for the happy result that awaited its conclusion.

My companions were also refugees from the persecutions of the Knights of the Lone Star—not on account of disagreement in politics or ritualistic forms, but because the doughty cavaliers had adopted an unwritten code, into which they had engrafted the principle of making booty of beauty, by possessing themselves of the wives and daughters of such as were not connected with the order, and who had not sufficient influence to protect their household gods against the assaults of *respectable scoundrels.*

These two men were possessed of wives, who, in the estimation of their husbands, were paragons of loveliness, and, it seems, others had admired; for, in some unaccountable manner, they had been spirited from their homes, and when their husbands followed up the traces closely, and had found a clue to their whereabouts, the cry of "Abolitionist" was raised against them, testimony proving their unsoundness on the nigger manufactured, and they were persecuted and pursued, till forced to fly to the swamps for their lives. And they were only two of a hundred they could mention who were similarly situated! In fact, there were six others, now in hiding with them, who had been pursued under circumstances almost identical with those related; and they proposed to conduct me to the rendezvous of the whole party, as soon as I felt able to proceed, with their assistance.

Finding myself in safe hands, with the prospect of a secure asylum, helped to strengthen my almost exhausted energies; and I was able, after a few trials, to stand on my feet, and, in a short time, to start off, with the assistance of my new friends, in the direction of their retreat.

Although the distance did not exceed three miles, it was broad daylight when we reached the place, which was away from any path or track, and protected by what would seem, to a casual observer, an impenetrable web of cactus. It was the place, of all such I ever saw, in which I would choose to secrete myself, did I wish to hide from all the world.

CHAPTER XVI.

THOUGHTS of Home—Preparations to Reach it—Another Disguise—Trail of
the Pursuers Discovered—Break Camp on a Venture—Embarkation under
a Salute not Bargained for—Sea Fight—Skillful Maneuvering of a Small
Craft—The Enemy Submerged, and all is over—Haven on a Rocky
Coast.

DURING the week I spent in that cave of the swamps, I heard
the tales of those other refugees; and, had I space for their horrible details here, I would present a record of crime and outrage
sufficient to make devils blush.

But the same miseries were in store for me, only varied by circumstances; and, as I am relating a personal narrative, for the in-
tegrity of which I am individually responsible, I am reminded to
follow the text.

I was very anxious to return to my home, and it seemed impossible to restrain my inclination to set out on the journey at once.
My companions, however, had discovered suspicious trails in the
swamps, and they would not listen to my plans, until the prospect
was brighter for leaving cover in safety.

It was agreed that, when I did leave, they would see me beyond
the jurisdiction of my pursuers in safety, or share my fate in a
contest with them, provided we were forced to this extremity.

I busied myself in preparations for my homeward journey, not
the least important of which was a thorough remodeling of my
dress, which I accomplished by ripping it apart, one garment at a
time, and dying it in a coloring liquid made by my companions
from herbs and barks.

A friend of my fellow refugees came out from Galveston, one
night, and by him I sent for several articles to complete my disguise and contribute to my comfort; and when it was finally an-

nounced that our party was ready to move, I had provided myself a costume in which my own wife would not recognize me. I was dressed to the character of the accomplished desperado, and accoutered properly for that role, cap-a-pie.

On the morning of the eighth day of my "short shute" experience, everything was in readiness to commence the homeward journey, and scouts were sent out to reconnoiter, so that, if the signs were favorable, we might go forth with the night, and the better preserve our *incognito* under cover of darkness.

A boat had been provided, with which to cross over to the mainland, and one of our party was sufficiently acquainted with the country beyond to act as a reliable guide.

It was near night when the scouts returned, and, much to our chagrin, their report was not favorable. They had seen no one, but, late in the day, had stumbled upon a carefully covered trail, which, without doubt, was fresh, and indicated the close proximity of quite a party of men. By following this trail to a considerable distance, they had discovered it full of eccentricities—dodging about hither and thither in the utmost uncertainty, but keeping its general course toward Lafitte's ruins.

Two miles from these ruins our boat was hid, and it almost seemed like madness to undertake to reach it as we had arranged. But after reasoning the matter all through, *pro* and *con*, our guide decided on the point that it might be just as dangerous at any other time, and perhaps the danger would increase with our stay there; it was therefore just as well to break up camp to-night and sally forth as to wait for a more favorable opportunity. Everything was made ready at once, all signs of recent occupancy of the cave destroyed, and at about two hours before midnight we commenced our silent march in the order of single file, through cactus undergrowth and tall chapparel, with the determination to escape from that Texan Hades or die in the attempt.

It was eleven miles to the boat. We were little more than four hours in making the distance; but in all that time not a word had been spoken by one of our party. Ideas were occasionally conveyed by preconcerted signs, but the business in hand was in no way interfered with; and had there been outside spectators of that night march they might have imagined us a company of gnomes, raiding on the perturbed ghosts of those who, in other days, were followers of the Pirate of the Gulf. Such was the picture to my own fancy, and I almost wondered why the great Lafitte did not marshal his grim hosts under the black flag, and come forth to give us battle.

We reached the river without accident, held a hasty consultation while the boat was brought out from its hiding place, and were just congratulating ourselves on our good luck, when—

Bang! bang! bang! ping! ping! ping!

Four or five bullets whistled about our ears, and lodged among the trees and rocks.

"Inter ther boat, quick," commanded the guide, "an' all lay flat. I'll sail her, fer ther tide's out, an' we'll float away like ther devil. All in; then away we go, and luck fer 'em as beats."

Although the firing had greatly confused us, we were in the boat and away before the guide had done speaking. The tide was strong, and, without exertion on our part, we were riding out toward the bay with the speed of the wind, all lying in the bottom of the boat. Our pieces were carefully examined and made ready for use, for we could now expect nothing but a vigorous pursuit, as we had no doubt that preparations were ample for following us up. The guide was on the lookout, making every effort to penetrate the gloom in order to give notice of the first symptoms of danger; but on we went for near an hour, and still no evidence of pursuit. Of a sudden Bill Davis, who had remained remarkably quiet since embarking, sprung to his feet and declared that he heard the sound of oars near by. They had a suspicious sound, as though they were muffled, but he "heerd 'em clus," he whispered, "an' we'd better lay low fer ducks."

"Sh! sh! oars in ther locks, an' shutein' irons ready," whispered the guide. "Thar am ther cusses on ther stab'rd bow, an' was lookin' for 'em on lab'rd shore. W'en I say 'ready,' pull fer 'em like devils; w'en I say 'all ready,' fire at ther heads, an' don't waste no ammunishun. Not a word, yer understan', and we'll beat 'em yit."

The strange craft was down the stream, pulling against the tide, and almost directly in our course. It was evident they did not see us; but we had no doubt of their character from the emphatic report we had just heard, and therefore were prepared to give the proper tone to their reception. When we had floated to within perhaps twenty-five yards of them, the command was given,

"Ready!"

Six heavy oars sprang into the rowlocks, and the boat almost leaped out of the water. The enemy was confused, and we heard the command,

"Boat about!"

Then came the sound of oaths, a mixture of threats and entreaties, the report of a pistol, as if by accident, and the hail,

"Boat ahoy!"

We made no response; but as the enemy's craft turned and lay across the current, our guide shouted,

"All ready!"

And the simultaneous discharge of seven rifles told how that order was understood. Yells of agony attested to its effect.

"Starn all, an' run 'em down," commanded the guide.

We were within ten feet of them, and their boat square across our course. Again six strong men bent to the oars, and our keel cut and shivered them as though they had interposed but a thread of tow to our progress. Another shriek of despair, a few spasmodic chokings as the salt sea foam entered the nostrils of the drowning wretches, and all was over. Away we sped again; still on the lookout, till we felt certain all danger of pursuit by that route was over, when we tacked for the shore.

Of course we could not calculate our bearings exactly, but by the light of the early dawn we ran into a small cove, on a rocky coast, and there awaited the developments of the full day to determine our future action.

CHAPTER XVII.

Inaccessible Harbor—Backwoodsmen ever ready with Resources—Perilous Ascent—Catastrophe to a Heroic Adventurer—He finds a Watery Grave—Up or Down—Desperate Efforts for Life, or Certain Death—Visions of Starvation—A Night of Horrible Suspense.

We found ourselves completely hemmed in by palisades of rock, with no means of egress with our boat, except by turning back on the course by which we came. Shoreward, the ledge rose, almost perpendicular, to a great hight, and at first glance it seemed impossible to find a foothold to assist in scaling the barrier; but it was decided, after due deliberation, that it would be madness to turn back, and that we must discover some other means of changing our base. The guide was miserably ignorant of this cove—never had heard of it—and was therefore inefficient. Bill Davis proposed sending out scouts, who would investigate the feasibility of scaling the ledge; and this plan was finally agreed upon, provided we could find a point on which to land the men. For this we searched several hours in vain, and were about despairing when one of the party found a tolerable fissure, about eight feet from the water, in the perpendicular rock, with a projection of the ledge some twenty feet above; and, with an alacrity of invention for which the backwoodsman and frontiersman are noted, he at once proposed to throw the "lead" over the projection in such a manner as to fasten it there strongly enough to sustain a man's weight on the line, and then climb to the fissure, or further, and make such observations as the position would allow. The plan was immediately put into execution. The line caught and secured without difficulty, and the man commenced the toilsome ascent unhesitatingly, and climbed to the jagged projection without accident. He reported a fair prospect, that there was room for one other, and requested that one of us keep him company. Bill Davis volunteered and climbed the rope with the agility of a monkey; but, by some untoward mishap, as he was endeavoring to gain a foothold on the ledge beside his companion, he slipped, reeled, and, after immense exertions to save himself, fell, head downward, into the seething waters! We expected to see him rise to the surface at once, and all eyes were upon the spot where he went under, but after watching for ten minutes, or more, with no signs of his reappearance, expectation gave place to fear, and we knew we would never look upon the face of that devoted man again. He was in eternity!

The situation was distressing, but those brave hearts knew no fear; and soon as it was known there was no further occasion to look for Davis, another volunteered to go up the rope. He made the point, safely, and then it was decided that those two proceed as far as possible in the ascent, and report their discoveries soon as practicable. Directly we saw the line drawn up, and then, after witnessing many fruitless attempts to attach it at a greater elevation, it was caught on a point we could not see, from our location, and the men were soon out of sight.

It was now late in the day, too late to expect any result from this reconnoisance till morning. Our provisions were getting short, and, to add to the general discomfort, the sky was suddenly overcast with black clouds, and without doubt we would be compelled to pass the night in a heavy storm. There were still six of us left in the boat, and we busied ourselves in making all possible provision to guard against the fury of the elements. Our craft was rocking to and fro, in unison with the dashing waves, for we had found no place to "tie up;" and it required the services of two oarsmen to keep us off the rocks. When the storm came, we were obliged to take turns at the oars, two at a time, while the balance sat on the boats' bottom. Thus we rode out the weary night, and the morning found us wet, sore, hungry and dejected.

With the early dawn, all eyes were turned to the rocky elevation, for we felt sure relief must come from the report of the scouts. Not a soul in sight, and after picking up and carefully dividing the few remnants of food yet left, we resolved to make an effort to hail our companions. Hallooing loudly several times, we at last distinguished a faint reply, and in a few minutes had the satisfaction of seeing one of them swing himself down to the projection of the ledge. He lowered the line very quickly, secured it, and then told us that we must hasten, for he had reason to suspect that himself and companion had been discovered by our pursuers, and if his suspicions were correct, we had no time to spare. By general consent, I took the lead, and, after much tugging and squirming, reached the first ledge. Its entire area was not more than five square feet; and, as I stood there, with nothing to steady myself by but the force of my own will, I did not wonder at the mishap of poor Bill Davis. When the scout loosed the fastening of the line and threw the lead around another jutting crag, at least thirty feet above where we were standing, and coolly bade me ascend, my heart misgave me, and I told him I could not. Deliberately drawing a pistol from his belt and pointing it at my head, he lowered his ugly face close to mine and yelled:

"Gwo up er down, God damn yer, quick!"

I lost no time in seizing the line, and then was done the tallest climbing of my life. When I was something like half way up, a huge bird flapped his monstrous wings within a foot of my head, gave a great scream, and seemed about to pounce upon me. It was the Lord's mercy that I did not drop into the sea from the effects of fright, but at that moment my eye caught a fissure in the rock, into which I thrust a foot and rested my tired energies. But a voice from below soon notified me to go ahead; and, gathering all my strength for the effort, I climed to the second projection without further accident. It seemed about five minutes before the scout reached me, and, without regard for my fatigue, he immedi·ately attached the line to a higher point and bade me ascend. I did not hesitate now, but seized the rope at once and did my best climbing; but had I not discovered a friendly hand extended to me from over the projecting ledge, I must have failed to reach the end of the line, for my hands were bleeding, my feet bruised, my head dizzy and my breath nearly exhausted. It was the hand of welcome reached forth by the other scout, who was waiting in nervous anxiety, to witness the escape from danger of myself and friends.

"Things is a gittin' interestin'," said he. Crawl along ther ledge, keerful, for we're spied shore, an' ther'll be hell 'fore long, fer *somebody*."

Following his direction, I moved along the table of the ledge, on my hands and knees, to a small cave, within which I found comfortable quarters. He then left me, to reconnoiter, but in a short time I was joined by one of my companions from the boat, and then another, until at length we were all in the cave safe and thankful. But we were tired and very hungry. The question of food was of great moment, and not one of us had the remotest idea of how and where we could obtain relief. One of the men estimated that we must be about five or six miles from the town of Summit, and proposed that some one be sent there with him for supplies, while the balance should seek much needed rest and repose. Arrangements were soon concluded, and the two set out, in fine spirits, promising to return with food soon as possible; and they were sure it would be in a few hours.

Time dragged heavily enough in that cave of the rocks. We sat there looking into each other's faces, too much occupied with our troubles to talk, too hopeless to endeavor to cheer each other. And as the dark hours passed, each one in its turn dissipating the last lingering hope, the despairing gaze with which we regarded each other was dreadfully frightful. But soon nature asserted her claims too emphatically to resist, and one by one we dropped to sleep. The poor man's heaven was ours.

I awoke in dread affright. Something, I knew not what, had happened; but my companions were all in confusion; the blackest darkness enveloped us, and no one knew the nature of the trouble. One was sure he had been awakened by the report of a rifle,— another, that a human voice was calling for help, while another was strong in the belief that our retreat had been discovered, and that our pursuers were even now investigating our position. But all was silent, and gathering ourselves into something like order, we awaited more tangible demonstrations. In the stillness of that dark night, unable to distinguish each other's forms through the gloom, or to even discover whether there were not foes in our very presence, mingling with, and preparing to overwhelm us, I experienced in the few moments of painful suspense that intervened between my forced awakening, and the discovery of the cause thereof, an intensity of agonizing fear that words are powerless to describe. God protect us from a repetition of such experiences.

CHAPTER XVIII.

Coveted Supplies Intercepted—Their Rescue at the Cost of Blood—Human Snakes—Feast Beside the Corpse of a Noble Scout—He Bequeaths His Body as a Decoy to Entrap the Murderous Band—His Death Terribly Avenged, and a Hecatomb of the Villains Follow Him to the Dark Waters— A Parley with One-sided Conditions—Again on the Tramp for Civilization— Arrival at the Crescent City.

"Ho, boys!"

Bang!

Whiz-z-sh—thud!

A yell, shrill and cutting,—an unearthly groan, and right in our midst, among the jagged rocks, there fell the body of a man, sprinkling those who stood near with his warm blood! Some one ventured to inquire,

"What's the matter?"

"Come clus, an' 'll tell yer," said he, in a weak voice. "We got ther fodder all reg'lar, tu Summit, an' Jack an' me wus a-cumin' back, an' we'd een'mos' brung in, wen we seed snakes, a *few*. They wus jist a layin' low, an' a watchin' out for us. Wen they seed we'd spied 'em, they let sliver, an' all on 'em fired tu onct, a hittin' Jack plum dead, an' wingin' me squar on ther knee jint. I pottered for the kiver, rapid, an' in a little bit wus a crawlin' through ther brush, holdin' ther fodder tight, for I knowed somebody'd be gittin' sharp fer a bite. Oh! I'm mos' gone, boys. Jist a drap o' whisky, an' mabbe I'll git through."

A flask was held to his lips, and he immediately revived."

"Wal, I got 'round to ther op'nin', by ther fust ledge," he continued, "an' thar I seed snakes agin', an' foun' I mus' lay low. They did'nt git a sight o' me, but I know'd they was suspicionin' ther trail, for they kep ther peepers turned this way all ther time. Wen it got dark, thort I'd give 'em ther slip, but my knee was

YE MORGAN KNIGHTS ON YE "DARK AND BLOODY GROUND."

11

powerful stiff, and I cud only crawl. Bin'by I lost ther bearins, an' arter standin' out an' standin' in a heap, ventured to holler. The dam snakes let sliver agin', but didn't hit. I diskivered tho', thet wan'nt lame as I thort, an got up an' run like mad. But I run squar into 'nother snake's nest, an' then they woun' me up, shore. They're har' jist on top of ther ledge, an' boys, it's a bad show. They don't know ther lead now, an' 'spect I'm feeding fishes; but put me 'way out on ther rocks, so's the'll see me wen they look over, an' then—then—oh, oh,—boys—I'm gone! Dave Thomas," he exclaimed, seeming to gather all his energies for a last effort, "ef yer ever see my wife again', poor girl, tell her, Dave, that I furgive, es I hope God will,—oh, cum clus, boys. Good—good bye!"

We lifted him up, and one of our party found a large bundle slung with a cord across his shoulders. It contained provisions, and nothing could have been more acceptable, but I am truly ashamed to record that the dying agonies of the faithful scout were at once disregarded, and we all fell to devouring the food he had lost his life in procuring! He showed no further signs of physical existence, however, and we sat there, occasionally munching the cakes and bread, till dawn of day. Our whispered conference was all of plans to escape, but we saw no promise of deliverance in anything but a bloody fight. We were well armed and knew how to use our weapons, but our foes doubtless had the same advantage, and without doubt outnumbered us largely.

With the early light, the dead body of the poor scout was placed on the extreme outer projection of the table ledge, as a blind. Dave Thomas had reconnoitered, and had found a pass from our place of concealment that would lead us out in a different direction from that taken by our unfortunate friends who made the trip to Summit. He was strong in the belief that we would escape by his route, the difficulties of which were only so many arguments in its favor, as he viewed it. We therefore determined to make our preparations and be off at once.

We loaded our rifles and pistols, stowed the remnant of food in our pockets, destroyed all evidence of our rendezvous there, and, with Dave in the lead, commenced the toilsome ascent. I brought up the rear, and, as I was turning the first point of the pass, thought I heard a voice behind me. Dodging quickly behind the rock, and peeping cautiously back, I saw two men bending over the dead scout and engaged in earnest conversation. This then was the advance guard of the enemy, and we had not made our movement a moment too quick; but it occurred to me that we were now in a position to defy them; so giving the signal for a halt, I at once communicated my discovery to the others, and we held council on the spot. The youngest of our party, whose father was also with us, was set to watch the movements of the " snakes," and he soon reported that they were rifling the pockets of the dead man, and preparing to throw him over the ledge.

" Thet thar must be ther sign tu sen' 'em arter him," said Dave Thomas; " you an' me, Jem, 'll du it. Stiddy, now, my boy, an' fer his head, shore. Ready! aim! stiddy now! Fire!"

The two scoundrels sprang from the ground with an unearthly howl, staggered blindly, and went whirling down that awful depth, occasionally torn by the jagged rocks, into the seething billows.of the Gulf. But those two shots were like sowing the dragon's teeth, for as the smoke cleared away, we saw that table rock filled with armed men, who came in wild confusion on the scene, and seemed greatly at fault because they did not find us there. But they were not long in discovering the pass, and crowded into it heedlessly, still in confusion. It was very narrow, so they were obliged to advance single file. It was understood that we reserve our fire till they reached the point, and that we then rise and fire simultaneously with our rifles, reserving the pistols for those who came next. As they neared us they seemed to gather a little caution, and some held back, but they were soon in fair position for a good aim, and the signal to rise and fire was given. Never was an order executed with more steadiness and precision, and every shot told. Six poor devils went tumbling over the ledge, each leaving the trace of a stream of blood in his wake, and on to his unhappy doom.

" Charge on 'em, before they hev time ter load," was the command.

And so they came charging on our position, thinking to take us at disadvantage, but the first who came clambering up to the point received a bullet from my revolver, between the eyes, and went as another prize to the sharks of the Gulf. Still they pressed on, and still we shot them down, keeping two of our number safe behind the point to load rifles and pistols that we might at no time be without the means of giving our pursuers a warm reception. It was a bloody season, lasting about an hour, when the enemy in sight were reduced to five men. A finger from my left hand had been torn away by a rifle ball, and two had pierced my hat, but my companions were all unscathed.

The enemy asked for a parley. Dave Thomas objected, strongly, and declared it was our duty to shoot them all down, quick as possible; but a majority of our crowd thought it no more than fair to grant their request, as we now outnumbered them.

"Stack your arms and come around the point," said I.

They hesitated, conferred a moment, and finally refused.

"Very well, then," I replied; "the game will go on again."

"Hold, a minute," shouted an old fellow, who had lost his hat in the general scramble, "and we will do as you command."

As they came around the point, I asked if they made up the entire balance of the party that was now pursuing us. They answered in the affirmative, saying that their original number was twenty-seven; that three had been killed in previous skirmishes, and nineteen in this.

"What do you wish, now?" I asked.

"We would like to retire from the fight," said the old gentleman, "taking our arms with us."

"Ah! just so," I replied. "Your party is very effectually whipped, and now you would like to march away with all the honors of war. We can not *quite* agree to that, but this is what we will agree to. In the first place, however, which one of your party is best acquainted with the country hereabout?"

The old fellow was indicated as most thoroughly posted.

"This, then, is what we will do," I continued: "We will bind your comrades here, hands and feet, securely, and leave them, while you must go with us as a guide. We shall keep your company for one day's journey only, and then you will be at liberty to return and release your friends. Resistance will do you no good, but may result in harm; so, your only course is, to submit peacefully."

The four men did object, nevertheless, and one resisted stoutly; but we soon had them secure, placed in as comfortable position as circumstances would allow, and then took up our line of march once more.

In about two hours we arrived at the town of New Washington, and sent one of our men in for food and whisky, both of which he readily obtained. At noon we crossed Cedar Bayou on an old flat-ing, we arrived at our destination. Here we remained for a time sufficient to recuperate our worn-out energies, and then set forward for New Orleans. It was necessary still to be strictly on our guard, for well we knew the tenacity with which we would be pursued, and how fearful would be our punishment if detected and captured. We arrived, however, safely at the Crescent City, thankful for our escape from the human hyenas who were so closely following us.

CHAPTER XIX.

REVOLUTION in the Order and a new Dispensation inaugurated—Disunion of the States the determined purpose of Traitors—Return to St. Augustine— Exciting Scenes—The Parson re-appears upon the Stage—Contemptible weakness of his Soul—He imparts most heart-rending intelligence. Wife and Child murdered and the Author desolate.

I WAS not in a frame of mind to make a long stop at New Orleans, and the generally unsettled aspect of affairs there, was not calculated to re-assure me. There was the same uncomfortable air of restraint that pervades all provincial barracks-towns, and many of the people seemed oppressed by anticipations of disaster—the forebodings of a frightful storm. Incidentally, I formed the acquaintance of a Knight of the Circle, who, from his position, was enabled to preserve some show of conservatism; and he informed me that there was a great revolution in the order; that Bickley was deposed, and an entirely new government inaugurated; and that those who resisted the authority of the revolutionists were summarily dealt with, even to the taking of life. This Robespierrean reign of terror had become general, and had already made itself severely felt in all the Castles and Hives; and this was but the overture of a programme of blood, for at a grand council of the Knights of the new dispensation, that had just concluded its deliberations at Charleston, an immediate separation of the slaveholding States from the North, had been determined on; and the argument had been ably defended that if Secession resulted in war, it would ceartainly be a success. The advocates of hostile demonstrations were largely in the majority, and the strange madness that usurped their judgments ruled the hour. When the public mind is imbued with such dangerous fanaticisms, thinking men will always fear the worst. My own thoughts were of my wife and child; my fears were all for them; and I, therefore, hastened to be with them, to perform, as love and duty bound me, the office of their protector.

On the morning of my arrival at San Augustine, I noticed the same untoward complexioñ of matters that had struck me at New Orleans. It was less than an hour past dawn, but I found the wharf crowded with excited wranglers, who did not confine a settlement of their difficulties exclusively to the force of words, but occasionally promulged the arbitrament of the prize ring, and left the black seal of their dissent broad upon the countenances of their antagonists. Men, young and old, were collected in little knots of six to twelve, all excited, and evidently intent on one point.

The pre-occupation of the crowd, and my disguise protected me from recognition; but as I was crossing the levee, the report of a pistol and a stinging numbness in the elbow of my right arm almost threw me off my guard, for I thought I was attacked. On looking around, however, it became evident that the luckless bullet had not been intended for me, so I moved forward with all possible haste, for fear I might have forced upon me other undeserved attentions. I did not wish to stop in the city, and was alone intent on reaching my home; but as I was passing through one of the least frequented streets that I had selected to escape observation, I was suddenly hailed by a familiar voice, and my old friend, Parson Taylor, saluted me with great cordiality.

"Really, brother Wright," he exclaimed, "this is a happiness, and a surprise. Where do you come from, and how came you here?"

I commenced to relate my story, when he excitedly exclaimed:

"Why your arm is completely soaked in blood. You are badly wounded, I fear, so come to me till we have it attended to."

A short walk brought us to the old man's house, and he immediately went to work for my relief. The bullet had shattered a bone, slightly, and was lodged in the fleshy part of the forearm, making it quite easy to dress the wound; and I was soon comfortable. After partaking of a delicious breakfast, I related my experience, from my escape in female dress, when I abandoned my fellow-prisoner to his fate, and stole his crape, up to the accident on the levee, that had just occurred; and never was auditor more thoroughly beside himself with surprise and painful emotion, than Parson Taylor, as he listened to my recital. Tears, profusely shed, atested the genuineness of his sympathy, and he wrung my hand in a very agony of grief, and continued for several minutes to ex- bibit evidences of the deepest woe. Finally he appeared calmer ; but I could scarcely credit the evidence of my sense of hearing, when he suddenly jumped up from his chair, and astonished me with these words :

"Would to God, brother Wright, you had been killed, or had died; anything, rather than have returned here! Do you know what has happened, and what fate is in store for you when it is known you have come back?"

"I know that I have done nothing wrong, and my duty to my family would bring me back, if I had no other motive. It seems you have overlooked a point that one would imagine should have your first attention. I wish to proceed to my home at once, and, after I am assured of the health and safety of my wife and child, I am prepared to meet any charge that may be brought against me."

"I feel that you have done nothing criminally wrong," said the old man, "and I know that the promptings of duty and affection have brought you here, only to be disappointed in—"

"WHAT?"

"Calm yourself, my dear friend, and summon all your fortitude, for it will require a stout heart to endure what has unfortunately fallen to my lot to relate to you. In order that you understand fully, it becomes me to go back to the time when we started for Galveston—"

"No, no! don't refer to that now, but tell me of my wife and child. They are first in my thoughts, because they occupy my heart; and when I hear that they are well and happy, I can listen to the relation of unimportant events. Tell me of them at once," I exclaimed, as I saw him troubled and hesitating, "tell me now, or I will go to them without further delay, and assure myself of the facts."

I arose to go forth.

"Sit down, Wright, and be calm," exclaimed the Parson, at the same time giving abundant evidence of his own lack of self-control by bursting into a flood of tears. His emotion was incomprehen- sible, and filled me with the gloomiest forebodings. I besought him to speak,—to tell the story in his own way, but to come to the point soon as possible, for suspense like mine was hard to bear. He spoke nearly as follows :

" I will not go back now to the point proposed, but explain my desire to do so at some other time. On my return from Galveston, I was told that you were dead, and having no means of assuring myself to the contrary, finally believed it. · I was also told that you caused the death of Judge Firman, which I, of course, emphatically denied; but I soon found that it was *part of a plot* to make this charge against you and *my life was threatened if I denied it again!* I am an old man, weak, nervous, and somewhat undecided, and have therefore been guilty of the great sin of hearing you repeatedly charged with the crime of MURDER without denying it, when I knew it to be false. Thus, I have assisted your enemies in branding you with a foul crime, of which, were your presence here known, you would be made to suffer the extreme penalty without the forms of trial. You must not be seen in the streets, even in disguise, for notwithstanding the great change in your appearance, I recognized you at sight, just as every one will who has known you intimately."

" But, my dear sir, there is nothing easier than to disprove this foul charge ; and it is my duty to myself and family to disprove it without delay. You will not refuse your evidence now as to the facts ?"

"We must be very circumspect, my friend. I am fixed in the belief that your appearance in public would be the signal for your immediate execution, without giving you an opportunity to produce evidence, and that, if you had opportunity, and proved your innocence beyond the shadow of a doubt, your fate would be the same."

" Does my wife know of this charge ? "

" She must have heard of it."

" Have you seen her recently ? "

" Not for several days."

" Had she heard that I was dead ? "

" Yes ! she had heard such a report, but I am told she did not credit it."

" You were told she did not ? Did she say nothing to you on the subject ? "

" No ! "

" Were she and my child in good health when you last saw them ? "

No reply.

" Parson Taylor, you must answer me this question, or I will go and ascertain in person.   I will not be kept in suspense."

" My dear friend, be calm.   I will answer anything in reason, and am pained to tell you that your family is not in health.   I beg of you not to question me further now, and I will soon tell you all."

" Answer me once more, in mercy ; are they dangerously ill ?"

" Oh, no! they're not ill at all,—that is, I think they are not now—but I am confused.   Really, friend Wright, you *must* excuse me—"

" No, sir!   I have already wasted too many words, and now *demand* the facts.   You tell me that my family is not in health, and that they are not ill.   How am I to understand so bungling a paradox?   In a word, tell me the truth without evasion, or it will be the worse for you, for I am getting desperately in earnest on this point, and shall not regard your office nor professions till it is settled.   Without equivocation or evasion," said I, rising in a threatening attitude, " what was the condition of my wife and child when you last saw them ?"

" My friend, you are excited, and can not endure an answer to that question, such as you demand, and, for God's sake, don't force me to answer you now.   Have some rest, calm your excited nerves, and then I will tell you all."

"This is madness.   You refuse to answer me, and I will go home, let the consequences be disastrous as you represent them; for I shall go wild if I remain longer in this suspense.   Do you still refuse a reply?"

" Well, WRIGHT, if I must tell you the truth prepare your mind for a terrible affliction.   Sit down and calm yourself, and I will tell you all."

"I shall not be calmer than I am now.   I am ready."

The old man looked at me tearfully, and was silent.

" I am ready; proceed."

"You promise to be calm ?"

"Yes !"

" It will require all your strength, for I never had more sorrowful news for a father.   *Your child is dead!*"

" *Dead? Dead?* old man; do you say that my Effie,—my darling,—that is my heart's blood, and the joy of my life, is *dead?* Effiie, dead?   Oh, it is cruel to say that; and as you hope for the

mercy of heaven, old man, tell me it is a lie,—a wicked fabrica-
tion,—a—anything but the truth. Say that you were instructed
to tell me this just to torture me,—oh, unsay those cruel words,
and I will bless you with my latest breath."

"I tell you what I know, of my own knowledge, dear friend.
Would it were not true; but you promised calmness, and you are
unduly excited. Now, do take some rest, for I have engagements
that call me out. When I return we will confer regarding your
plans for the future; and you may rely on my friendship in every
event."

"God have mercy on my poor heart! I have now drank of the
bitter cup, truly; but tell me of my wife. How does she bear this
affliction?"

"When I return, Wright, we will talk of that," replied he, in a
choking voice.

His tone and manner startled me, and I exclaimed :

"Tell me now, in mercy. I can bear the worst—all."

"Poor soul," said he, abstractedly; "you know not what you
ask. Would that some other had my task to perform. Nerve
yourself to receive a more painful announcement than I have made,
for the worst is yet to come."

"Then, my wife, too, is dead! Is that what you would say?
Oh, it is! it is! I see it in your looks; I know it! My God! do
I deserve so much misery? Now they may do their worst—I care
not. Do you say they will hang me? They are welcome, and I
will go to my fate as to a feast. Dead? Lucy and Effie, both?"
And then I raved wildly, as I was afterward told, and did many
insane acts, to the great detriment and chagrin of the worthy
Parson and his family. During the long weeks I was sick under
that hospitable roof, I was cared for tenderly, and I am deeply
grateful; but, at last, when they permitted me to leave the bed
and crawl about the house, I found that I was a spirit-broken,
heart-deserted, old man, at thirty years. There was little of value
left to me in life!

Wife and child both gone! Would that I had gone with them!

CHAPTER XX.

CONSPIRACY to accomplish the Author's Death—Villainy under the guise of Friendship—A high-souled Yankee Wife nobly defends her Virtue and baffles the purposes of a Southern Knave—His murderous attempt upon her Life—Poisoning of her Child—The Mother soon follows her to the Realms of Bliss.

ON the plea of my unsoundness to the cause, a conspiracy had been planned against me before I started for Galveston, with the intention of embroiling me in such a manner with the Texan Knights that I could not escape alive. Had my companions been left to follow out their instructions without hindrance, such would doubtless have been the result, and hence the easy credence accorded to the report of my death. It pains me to write of the real object of this conspiracy, but it is an important link in this history, and the truth must appear.

Among my pretended friends at San Augustine, was one Tallbot, who professed an extraordinary regard for the welfare of myself and family. He was the smoothest villain I ever saw—handsome, polite in all the *forms* that word describes; cautious, deliberate, scheming. He came often to my house, at first on my invitations, for I had always judged men hastily, and my first impressions of this man were favorable; but my wife did not like him, and the more she saw of him, the less he shared her esteem. He either did not notice, or, with the nonchalance of a thorough-bred *roue*, affected not to see, her changed manner, that constantly marked the degree of disfavor into which he had fallen; but, as voluntary attentions to his comfort became fewer and less noted, with the shrewdness of an old tactician he constantly paraded his claims to favor, by noisily disavowing and ignoring them. I could not ac-

count for Lucy's persistent dislike, and her unusual reticence was
mysteriously uncomfortable; but after this state of things had continued for several months, she began to exhibit signs of a rebellious
disposition, and pointedly requested that I would not again invite
Tallbot to see us. It then seemed time for me to ask for explanations, and she informed me that she had long ago discovered my
friend was not a gentleman, although his ordinary speech and
manner would seem to mark him as such. That he had indulged
in language to her that his manner had interpreted in a very offen-
sive sense, and she was sure his designs were anything but honorable. But I was slow to believe; in fact, saw nothing to really
condemn; and joked Lucy on her Northern prejudices, puritanical
education, and remarkable quickness at noticing defects in everybody but her husband. I was wrong, and she was right; and every
woman is right in similar discoveries. God has implanted among
the perceptive organs of every female a faculty that instinctively
sounds the alarm at the first indication of an attack on her virtue,
and woe to her who disregards its warning voice!

Tallbot now came uninvited, and so after that I began to feel it
an abuse of hospitality, therefore did not always give him a cordial
welcome. He was doubtless well enough aware of the change in
my manner, but had too much command over himself, or was too
intent on his object, to make a corresponding change. He had
probably played the *role* too often to be "put out" in any
sense.

To this *friend* was I indebted for my appointment on the commission to regulate the Galveston Knights; and his genius has
credit for the scheme to murder me. I found him at my house on
the night of my appointment, and he was very demonstrative in his
congratulations.

"You are the man for the emergency," said he, with his bland-
est manner, "and I am sure the interests of the order could not be
in safer keeping. All rely on your firmness to push the great objects of the commission, and that there will be no compromises."

He had already secretly joined the New-Lights, and was therefore politely counseling me to do what he knew would cost me
my life!

I am indebted to my friend Taylor for the principal facts that
make up the balance of the chapter. I had been absent but four
days, when "*brother* Tallbot" rode to·my house in great haste, and

abruptly informed my wife that I was dead! Without giving her
time to reply, he told her he was much pressed for time just then,
that the particulars of my death had not been received yet, but
soon as they were, he would send them to her. Riding hurriedly
off, he left poor Lucy almost distraught with the astounding intelligence. Her distraction was soon tempered by doubts, however;
and the questionable characteristics of Tallbot, enabled her to divine
his motives for giving currency to such a report; but love must be
perfectly satisfied,—so she made hurried preparations, and called
on my attorney in St. Augustine. He had just received a similar
announcement of my sudden demise, without particulars, and was
therefore incapable of offering any words of comfort to my poor
wife. So she retraced her steps in sadness, and returned to her
home in something like a realization of a great and overpowering
misery. For two days and nights she ate not, slept not. On the
third day, came Tallbot with a neatly fashioned lie, detailing all
the particulars of my fate, and loudly eulogizing the dead; and for
a time Lucy forgot the *villian*, and treated him as a friend. He
stopped to dinner, and almost exceeded himself in efforts to remove
the disagreeable impressions he had previously made. His words
of condolence were so ingeniously simulated, it is little wonder that
the poor woman was partially thrown off her guard. He prelonged
his visit late after night, and when the servants had retired, he attempted an act to make devils blush!—Seizing a pistol, she aimed
it steadily at his head, and the coward ran from her; but with true
courage and commendable judgment, she attempted to fire on him.
The cap exploded without igniting the charge. Then he supposed
her at his mercy, and turned back; but she was ready, for the revolver was fully charged; and bringing him within range, she fired
deliberately, sending a bullet plowing through his smooth cheek,
and tearing away a piece of an ear in a fashion that will leave him
a monument of woman's vengeance till the day of judgment.

Tallbot howled and danced with rage and pain; but soon footsteps
were heard, as the alarmed household commenced to hurry toward
the parlor. Rushing up to Lucy, he dealt a powerful blow with his
clenched fist upon her head, that felled her to the floor; and then
dashed through the window, just as two negro men were entering
the room. One of them sprang after him, but too late, for he had
gained his horse, and was galloping rapidly away before Jem
reached the gate.

When they raised my dear wife from the floor, her face was covered with blood. The poor slaves were almost beside themselves with terror, but the women finally removed her to a bed, and a physician was summoned. He examined her injuries very gravely, and expressed no hope for her recovery; but next day she rallied, and conversed several hours with friends that called. And so for several days, although her attacks of delirium were growing daily more and more severe.

Late one evening an old woman, or a devil in disguise, was seen at my gate, with my little daughter in her arms. The child was immediately brought in by one of the negroes, but the old woman had given her some pleasant confections, which she continued to eat and enjoy highly. They were poisoned, and before the light of another dawn, that darling of our hearts had joined her sister angels in Paradise.

Who shall paint the dark misery that now filled the heart of my devoted Lucy? Who shall say that there is a more dreaded hell than the Knights of the Circle can make here on earth?

On the day after the murder of my little one, Parson Taylor returned to his home, having been released from captivity in Texas. Hearing of the state of affairs at my house, he hastened thither, and was fortunate in finding my wife able to converse understandingly. He informed her that the report of my death was premature, and doubtless unfounded, and cheered her greatly with hopes of my speedy return; but it was plain to him she would last only a few days. He performed the last sad rites over my little girl, and made a grave for her among the flowers she loved, in the house-yard that had been her play-ground. And regularly, every day, he called to talk and pray with my dying wife, till near a week had passed, when he was one day summoned hastily to her bed side, and found her almost expiring.

"Bury me beside my child," said she, feebly, "for I am going now. Tell Edmund, for I feel he is yet alive, that my latest breath was spent in prayers for him."

And then the soul of one of the loveliest women that ever blessed this cold world with her presence, winged its flight to the realms of bliss. Oh, my sacrificed wife! my angel child. My heart lies between those two graves in the Peninsular State!

CHAPTER XXI.

TERRIBLE Scene of Domestic Desolation—A Heart-broken Parent—Sorrow among the Tombs—Progress of Escape—Arrival at Charleston—Soldan of Galveston Castle holds a high position in the Army of Rebeldom—Again in a Loyal State—Incidents in the Quaker City—Traitors in the North and their Disloyal Purposes—Northern Lovers of the Union, beware of the insidious wiles of Villians in your midst—Is Copperheadism Democracy ?—Conclusion.

AND now my home was truly desolate, for after the assassin came the incendiary ; and my loved ones were scarcely in their graves, before the torch was put to the buildings, and everything devoted to destruction.   Negroes and stock were killed and stolen ; furniture destroyed ; family plate and all the heir-looms of all the generations that had preceded me, confiscated; and all the cares of the household turned over to indiscriminate ruin !   But I must not look back, for my brain is reeling and my heart bleeding the moment I allow my mind to recur to those scenes.

Nearly three months I was kept in hiding at Parson Taylor's; but one night near the witching hour, the desire to visit the ruins of my home, and the graves of my loved ones, possessed me so strongly that I resolved to venture forth.   Leaving the house without discovery, I quickly traversed the well-remembered road, and arrived safely at the scene of my former happiness.   The moon was shining in all her beauty, but on what desertless misery did she look down !   How shall I describe the pain, the heart-crushing agony of that hour, as I seated myself near those irregular mounds and gazed upon the sod that buried my dead hopes away down in the cold earth?   The ruins of my worldly possessions were as naught—I gave them no heed, no care ; for between myself and those heaps of earth, there was a connecting link that grappled on

12

my heart, and drew it from me, bleeding and sore, far down into those dark graves! And there it still rests, and will remain forever!

I was awakened from a long revery by the red light of a distant fire, that I afterward learned was the destruction of the estate of a dissenter to the monstrous doctrines of the Circle. But it was time for me to hasten away, and with one more look at the resting-place of my wife and child, I returned to the Parson's, and betook myself to repose. I have not looked upon those graves since—but now, thank God! the glorious flag of the free is again waving in Florida, and I will soon see them again!

Another week has passed, and by the help of friend Taylor, who, although a semi-rebel, was moved to assist me on account of my sufferings, my arrangements are complete for escape to the North. I again disguised myself in female apparel, and passed, sometimes as a beggar, sometimes as a fortune-teller, through scenes and adventures enough to fill a volume. I arrived in Charleston the day after the surrender of Sumter, and there I saw and recognized the Soldan of the Galveston Castle, who had murdered Judge Firman. He held a high position in the army of the rebels, and his name has now become historical; but I never hear it without connecting it inseparably with one of the darkest deeds of blood that ever stained the records of crime!

On the 3d day of June, 1861, I arrived in the city of Philadelphia, and made my story known to a couple of gentlemen, who immediately interested themselves in my behalf, and procured me a presentable wardrobe and a liberal supply of money. I was then requested by them to go to a popular hotel, and register myself by name and residence, and watch the result. I watched for several days faithfully, and almost despairing of making the wished for discovery, when one evening a gentleman approached and called me by name. I was greatly surprised, for he was an utter stranger; but he explained at once that he saw my name on the book, and that the clerk had pointed me out. After a few common-place remarks, he touched on the war, and without waiting to learn my sentiments, denounced the action of the administration and the North, in emphatic terms. While talking, he used words and signs that I could not fail to recognize, and therefore, agreeably to instructions, answered them. He proved to be a King of a Lancaster

Hive, and Jeff Davis never owned a more servile hound than this " cur of low degree."

What I learned from this Pennsylvania renegade is utterly worthless, except as proving the animus of the Copperhead movement, and it is therefore sufficient to record that he marked out for me in skeleton, the entire programme of the Copperhead party, as it has since developed itself, then and there; and stated boldly that its objects were to encourage the rebellion, and cripple the efforts of the administration to put.it down! And I probably need not go farther into this subject, than to simply add, that I have since visited all the Hives and Castles but one, that were then at work in the Northern States, and that I have found them in every instance, made up, directed, and controlled by men who express the same detestable sentiments. The evidence in every case, has been sufficient to convince me that those men are the prime movers in the Copperhead faction, leading away honest men, by false professions, from their loyalty, and seeking to destroy the blood-bought heritage of our fathers; but I am forced to admit that the evidence in every case, as I am prepared to furnish it, might not be sufficient to convince my readers, especially were it against their will to be convinced; and I am therefore prompted to caution all parties, all men and women, against saying anything, doing anything, or thinking anything in opposition to the present administration of our government, till the war is closed, and every indication of a rebellious movement in our land crushed out.

This advice may seem strange to this people, but if we would save ourselves from the rule of the Order whose designs I have imperfectly sketched in this volume, we must make every sacrifice to resist its encroachments, for it is great and powerful, and will carefully reckon our weaknesses for its profit. Men of the North, be not deceived, the wolf is now at your very door, and thirsting for the blood of those you love!

In the recent State elections, when Copperheadism made itself prominent under the sheep's clothing of Democracy, thousands of loyal Democrats were basely deceived, and acted with the enemy. Are their eyes yet opened to the truth of their position, or have they confounded Copperheadism and Democracy? I glory in the name of Democrat. Thank God, I am not of the Copperhead stripe!

I have refrained, as much as possible, from the relation of personal experiences, irrelevant to a proper exposition of the subject in hands, and have rather erred in the omission of particular matters, rather than risk tiring the reader with what he might view in the light of unwarrantable prolixity; but, should the public view this little work with any considerable degree of favor, it will be followed by another of more pretensions, in which the author will detail scenes and incidents that came under his personal observation, and in the experience of friends and acquaintances at the South, that, to say the least, will repay perusal.